THE
KING'S
COMMANDER

A LEGENDS OF MERIA NOVEL

CECELIA
MECCA

THE KING'S COMMANDER

CECELIA MECCA

ALTIORA
Press

THE KING'S COMMANDER

Copyright © 2020 by Cecelia Mecca

Edited by Angela Polidoro

Cover Design by Najla Qamber Designs

Photography by Wander Aguiar

All rights reserved.

CHAPTER ONE

VANNI

Castle d'Almerita, Kingdom of Meria
"They're all dead."

So the rumors are true?

"I came right away," I say as the man I've served my entire life buries his head in his hands. One by one, the others pile into the throne room behind me. King Galfrid doesn't even seem to notice. Standing, he moves to the window. I wait with the other members of the Curia as the most powerful man in the kingdom slips his hands over his bowed head in complete despair.

"Vanni?" the king's chancellor whispers to me. I shake my head. This moment deserves silence. Reverence.

Friends. Brothers in arms. We've lost so many this day.

Including the king's son and successor.

A warm breeze drifts in from the open windows. In the chambers below us, only small, shuttered openings and arrow slits puncture the castle walls. A safety precaution. But we're so high above the earth up here, only the sea is our witness.

1

Bright orange and crimson silk hangings flutter in the breeze as our king stands still next to them.

The whole Curia is now assembled. When the heavy wooden doors are closed behind the last of us, my liege finally turns to address the men assembled before him.

"The rumors are true. The boat sank this morn, one survivor living to tell the tale."

My chest swells with hope—could Prince Matteo have survived after all?—but in the very next breath he dashes it.

"The captain's son lives. As does my nephew, who apparently imbibed too much drink last eve and lasted only a few moments at port before he disembarked. All others perished in the sea not long after the Oryan left port last eve. According to the boy who washed ashore clinging to a piece of wood"—his voice cracks—"its port side struck a submerged rock and the ship quickly capsized and sank."

We all cross ourselves and mutter words of sorrow for the boy and the implications of Galfrid's nephew having survived when his son did not.

Matteo. A wave of nausea hits as I think of the prince, the boy who became a man alongside me. The strong and thoughtful son of our king. How could he be gone when just days ago we trained together, Matteo as skilled a swordsman as any.

I push aside thoughts of everyone I knew on board . . . and the fact that I was originally supposed to go with them.

Galfrid needs us now, more than ever. And I live to serve him.

"We will mourn tomorrow," he says. The king's voice is strong, but his eyes betray him, at least to me. While all of those present serve at the pleasure of the king, I alone was raised by him. My heart bleeds for him, and for the kingdom.

The loss of Prince Matteo weighs heavily on us both. Despite my intention to focus on the king's words, I cannot help but think of him. His last moments. His promising future as the king Meria needed. Though not for lack of trying, the king and queen of Meria have produced just one child, and he is now lying at the bottom of the Merian Sea, along with two hundred of our most skilled warriors. The heir to the kingdom is dead.

The king addresses me. "You will go to him. Tell him of what's happened here. Bid him to return."

Silence follows his words. None, including me, need to be told of whom he speaks.

I nod.

"He will not come." Thomas voices what each of us already know.

But Galfrid doesn't waver. "He must."

Pinning his hopes, the kingdom's hopes, on the journey I'm about to take, the king begins to issue further orders. As the Curia, his most trusted advisors, discuss the further implications of this unfolding disaster, I'm already considering who to take with me, whether to journey by land or sea, and what to say when I arrive. As the first commander of the Curia, I should at least be able to gain an audience with him. But will he listen? Will he return with me?

"What say you, Vanni?"

I'd not been listening.

"Apologies, sire."

Though not temperamental, the king is not a patient man. At his scowl, Ren, Galfrid's second commander, repeats the question.

"Will we mount another attack on Edingham?"

It was an easy decision.

"We have a more imminent threat."

The other members of the Curia proceed to argue with each other as if the king hadn't just lost his child. Some remind Galfrid of the reason he agreed to the attack. Or the

3

preparations we've been undergoing for months. Others agree with me, that the king's nephew will waste no time gathering support to lay claim to the greatest prize in Meria.

Heir to the crown of our great kingdom.

"Enough," the king says, and the rest quiet. We all know one man's opinion matters more than the rest.

"Edingham will have to wait until Vanni returns."

All eyes turn to me.

There are just seven people in all of Meria who know the king has a bastard son. Six of them are in this room. The seventh? The king's wife, who insisted the babe be sent away.

"He must come." I can easily read the king's expression. Hidden beneath his regal bearing and trimmed white beard is a look of gut-wrenching grief and worry. I've never seen him like this, and he does not wear the emotions easily. But there's only one comfort for a king who cares about his kingdom above all else: to know his crown will pass down to a worthy man. His nephew, whom none in the Curia like, does not meet that description.

He must not become the heir. I will ensure it.

CHAPTER TWO

AEDRE

*M*urwood End

God be praised, it is, at least, a blessedly sunny day. We have so few of them here, even in summer, and the sun is a necessary part of my plan.

"Is that jasper?" Anna, the cobbler's wife, peers over my shoulder. "Tis a most unusual color, no?"

It is. Which is the precise reason I've choosen it.

Whatever she may think, the cobbler's wife does not need her husband to fall in love with her again. She needs to see herself as *Anna*, a person whose worth is not dependent on anyone else. I've visited her so often, she's given me three new pairs of shoes as payment, yet she still refuses to heed any of the advice I offer.

My amma says to save the jasper for when I have no other hope for healing. With luck, this will bring Anna some peace.

"Aye, 'tis so for a reason," I say.

Then, just as the sun hits the deep red stone, faint lines of grey appear. She gasps and leans closer. Clutching the stone to my chest, I mentally recite the words my grandmother taught me.

Spred manns Hoc, fide tum boll. Boll tum fie, Hoc manns Sprend.

I open my hand, the lines now gone. "Take it."

Anna looks at my hand as if it's poisoned. A familiar tug in my chest reminds me that even the most ardent supporters of my practice have been taught to mistrust it. But Anna has known me since childhood, and she gingerly takes the stone.

"Hear me, and this shall be our last meeting."

As always, she glances down the road at the overgrown path that leads away from Murwood End. Her cottage sits on the northernmost edge of the village. Beyond us, the road leads away from the only home I've ever known to lands I'll likely never see, if my father has his way. It is safe for my kind here. For me and Amma, for our ancestors. Not so beyond the Loigh Mountains.

We attend to each other once again.

Taking her hands in mine, I say the words that are more important than any spell.

"You must love yourself above all others. When you can do that, your fate will begin to change course."

Is she ready to listen to my words?

I'm unsure, so I squeeze her hand shut with the talisman inside. "If you've any doubts, put this in the sunlight as I've done today. Squeeze it as a reminder of my words, and consider them well."

She nods with the same solemnity I had when Amma first showed me this spell. I asked Amma, more than once, if it works because of the way the sun strikes the stone, the words I utter or the Garra blood that runs through my veins, but she always answers the same way. Does it truly matter? I suppose it does not, but sometimes, like today, I wish I knew the answer.

"You are not the cobbler's wife. You are Anna. Daughter of a fierce voyager and the kindest soul in these parts. Aye?"

"Aye," she whispers.

"'Twas weakly done."

"Aye," she says again, but her voice is still not adamant enough for my liking.

"I cannot hear you," I lie.

"Aye," she says more loudly this time. For now, I'm satisfied.

I release her hands. "You will have no need of me after today."

It is more of a hope than a prediction, but it wouldn't help Anna to tell her so.

"How can I repay you, Lady Aedre?"

I open the door to leave, ignoring her question as I want no more payment. Movement outside catches my attention, and my eyes narrow in disgust. The men are still a ways off, too far for me to count them, but I spy the flag they bear before they dip into the valley, their party no longer visible. To these men, I am mistress and not lady. Southerns have little respect for Garra or the titles bestowed on me and my ancestors. Or so I've been told.

"'Twas the Merian king's flag, was it not?" Anna asks.

"Aye."

"We should wait inside." Anna pulls my arm, but I refuse to go back with her.

I will hide from no man, most especially those sent by a king I do not recognize.

"My lady, come inside with me." She tugs again.

Living at the edge of the village, Anna is rightly leery of strangers. She knows the guardhouse defending our village only offers so much protection. Wayward Highlanders and thieves can easily make their way to Murwood End. But these men are neither.

They are worse.

"Nay." I disentangle myself from her. "I will not."

My father's voice rings in my ears.

Stubborn girl.

I am that, and more.

But then I notice Anna's expression. She wishes to go inside but feels beholden to stay with me. And so my feeble stand comes to an end. I allow her to push me into the straw-thatched cottage, and despite the warm day, Anna proceeds to close every wooden shutter. After she lights a candle, the modest furnishings once again come into focus. We move toward one of the shutters and wait.

"You have always been so brave, Lady Aedre," she says softly.

My father would call it something very different.

"Garra have been so for centuries," I whisper back even though we are very much alone.

"What do you suppose the Garra of Meria are like? Or Edingham?"

I'd not know firsthand as I've never left Murwood End. "My grandmother says we are all very much the same, no matter the kingdom. Our goal, to learn and share all we can of love and its healing properties. She also says Garra do not practice openly in the capital."

"How fares Lady Edrys?"

"She is well."

When I left, my amma had been perched just outside the forge's window watching the sea with one eye, my father with the other. Surely Father knew she sat there to distract herself, but he played along. In addition to being a skilled blacksmith and an overprotective father, he is one of the kindest men in all of Murwood End, more tolerant of his mother-in-law and daughter than he pretends.

"I left her sitting outside the forge awaiting the ships' return."

Two of them were due to arrive any day now. It is a favored pastime of the villagers, predicting the return of the Voyagers.

"Do you hear that?"

I did. The slow, steady beat of horses' hooves pounding the dry earth.

We peek out from the shutters as the sound intensifies.

The tips of their gold and red banners become visible before the men themselves. They slow as they spot us. Anna's breathing becomes erratic, and I lay a hand on her shoulder.

"Bastards, aye. But not likely here to harm us." I keep the venom from my voice. "We are just a curiosity to them."

I squint, attempting to calm myself as much as my companion.

They're too far away for me to hear their words. It doesn't help that all four are helmed, but I watch as the leader, clearly marked as such by his bearing, grasps his helmet and pulls it off.

If I could've controlled the swift intake of breath, I would have. Because I've clearly shown my hand.

"A rightly handsome man," Anna whispers, echoing my thoughts.

Nay, more than handsome. Regal, almost. One who knows his worth. His hair nearly shoulder length, as I'd expect of a Merian, though slightly wavy and as dark as mine, his skin touched by many a summer's day. When he turns our way, I silently thank Anna for having pulled me inside. If I'd been out there, he would have witnessed my unwitting reaction to him. I watch as he signals for the others to move once again, confirming my suspicion that he is indeed their leader.

"Aye," I finally agree as they pass. Anna tosses the door open, and we step outside.

"Why are the king's men here?" she wonders aloud, again echoing my thoughts.

"I do not know, but it does not bode well for Murwood End."

Or for me.

CHAPTER THREE

VANNI

"*S*hall I take Dex, my lord?"

"Nay."

My squire doesn't question the reason. He knows it pacifies me to care for my own horse, and at this moment, I am in need of pacifying. We'd considered the possibility Master Aldwine might be out to sea. He is, after all, a Voyager. What we didn't consider is that none seem to know, or be willing to tell us, where he went or how long he'll be gone. Now all we can do is wait.

"I'll be along," I tell him and the others. Three men in total including Christopher, Thomas, and my loyal friend Salvi, more than I'd wanted to bring, but the king insisted. Murwood End does not pose much of a danger. The small hamlet tucked behind the Loigh Mountains along the northernmost tip of the island is home to a fiercely independent people. Isolated by the mountains we've traversed over the past days, they are better known for avoiding battles than engaging in them.

For years this place remained empty until the distant relatives of Lord Bailor, a current resident of Murwood End, sailed here from Hempswood in Meria. Weary of the politics regarding the splitting of the kingdom, he settled here. Those that later joined his family and their men were given one edict . . . to serve neither king. To this day they claim allegiance to neither place.

Since then the Voyagers have preferred to sail north for trade, even though those routes are longer and more dangerous than sailing south to Meria or Edingham. And though Voyagers have been accused of atrocities beyond our shores, most agree the tales are just that. Stories and nothing more. What matters is that these people are not, by all accounts, dangerous to me and my men. Though from the looks we've been receiving, I doubt my sword will remain sheathed.

After tending to Dex, the inn's stable boy as suspicious of me as the rest of the locals, I make my way toward the docks. The year before my parents died, I journeyed to this place with my father and his men. We took the usual route, past the Bay of Sindridge and up the east coast. When we came to the Cliffs of Murh, I struggled to keep from staring in awe. My father's stalwart retainers showed little emotion, however, and I was ashamed of my reaction.

The smell of salt air and fresh fish is somehow slightly different than back home, even though both are on the coast. It is a wonder to me we share the same land. There are fewer smiles and warm embraces. Darker clothing but lighter skin. I suspect I'd be known as an outsider even without the mark of the king on my breastplate.

But one thing we have in common with these people is a love for the sea. Unlike the Highlanders and mountain men, both Voyagers and Southerners, as they call us, survive on the bounties the sea brings.

Following a path along the docks back toward the inn, where we'll await Master Aldwine's return, I stop and watch as a fisherman wearing a brown leather apron hauls his catch across the planks. He tosses a net up to a similarly adorned woman, and together they call orders to those still aboard the ship.

Another difference between us. I know of no women captains in Meria.

"Does the sight of a woman in charge of her own ship startle you so?"

I smell her before I even see her, the scent of lavender replacing all else. I turn and nearly lose my footing on, well, nothing. We stand on a dry dirt path that leads to the docks, nothing to become unbalanced over, except the sight of her.

"A Garra," I blurt before thinking. The bright diamond on her nose identifies her.

I've met only one before, a woman who lives deep in the woods where the Terese River splits into two. All know she resides there, but few visit her for healing. I know of her only because Galfrid asked that we protect her. But this woman, the spectacularly beautiful, clearly defiant woman, stands before me with the small piercing in her nose conspicuous to all.

"So the rumors are true?" she asks.

"Rumors, my lady?"

"They say the Merian court is filled with men all praising each other for their esteemed maleness."

An interesting depiction of my people.

"They say the Voyagers are willful and defiant," I counter.

"And proud of it," she responds. "I've also heard the king loves himself above all and his men have difficulty deciding who they adore more, him or themselves."

This Garra is bolder than any woman I've ever met. For a man accused of smiling little, I do so now, more broadly than in recent memory.

"I'd not heard that bit of folklore before. But 'tis true," I say.

"Why are you here?"

The question is flung at me like an insult. Instead of answering, I watch as the sun strikes the diamond in her nose, making it sparkle. It was always curious to me that this special group of healers, so hated by the Church, would choose to mark themselves so outwardly. Some call them witches, but most agree, connected by blood and taught by their ancestors, Garra are nothing more than highly skilled healers of the heart. The others I've heard of live in seclusion, in caves and huts deep in the woods, but this woman makes no excuses for herself.

"Why are you not hidden?"

Her laugh is not a dainty one, like the women at court. It is hearty and deep, though not at all amused.

"You've much to learn, Southerner."

For all of this Garra's bravado, she speaks to me for a reason. And I'd know that reason before returning to my men. The call of seagulls drowns out my next words, so I wait until they pass to repeat myself.

"Southerner. King's man. Call me what you'd like, my lady, but it is you who approached me, not the other way around."

Her intelligent eyes narrow. "I saw how you looked at her, as if she was a puzzle to solve."

If there is a puzzle to be solved here in Murwood End, it is not the ship captain but the woman standing before me.

"We've no female ship captains in d'Almerita."

It's an honest answer, but she clearly dislikes it.

"Or in Meria," she says, flinging the fact at me like an insult.

"True enough."

"And how many women serve in the King's Curia?"

"None."

"You ask why I'm not hidden? Perhaps you ask the wrong questions."

Her words echo a sentiment I've heard back home—a choir of voices that has grown louder since Edingham crowned their first queen. But none have ever spoken to me quite so openly, so brazenly, as this woman. I goad her, knowing I should not.

"'Tis not the Merian way to insult strangers. But I've been told Voyagers have formed their own traditions."

"Ha! Been told? Have you not been so far north before?"

"Have you been to the other side of the mountains?"

The way she straightens her shoulders is answer enough.

"I am a mere blacksmith's daughter, not a man who represents a king. Unlike you, who are so well traveled but seem only to know the customs of those who reside in the lofty castle walls of d'Almerita."

My jaw clenches. I've faced opponents who've flung worse insults at me. Stared down well-armed soldiers intent on ending my life. Yet somehow this woman has inflamed me more than all of them combined. I nearly say something I'd surely regret, instead settling for a simple question. "What is your name?"

Her eyes narrow.

"You're correct—I'm the king's representative. If that means 'tis my responsibility to know all in the kingdom, I'd start with learning your name."

Despite her low opinion of me, I bow and introduce myself.

"Lord Vanni d'Abella, Curia Commander to King Galfrid of Meria."

Enjoying her momentary look of surprise, I add, "And I am indeed a stranger to these parts. I've been to Murwood End just once, as a boy, with my father."

When her chin rises, I'm sure my Garra will not reciprocate, but she surprises me.

"Lady Aedre, daughter of Dal Lorenson, descendant of Athea."

Athea, the first Garra.

The one who broke our kingdom, if the church is to be believed.

I let the name slip from my tongue. "Aedre, you may call me Vanni."

She is unimpressed that I've offered her leave to use my given name. In fact, I am certain very little impresses Aedre, daughter of Dal Lorenson, descendant of Athea.

Myself included.

CHAPTER FOUR

AEDRE

I should walk away.

We are healers, little one. Healers of the heart.

My grandmother taught me of love and attraction. When our ancestors' remedies are needed, and when they are not. She taught me to trust myself, trust the knowledge of my ancestors and to pass on the belief in oneself to every person who will listen. Against my father's wishes, she taught me enough to know that Lord d'Abella is dangerous to me, however much I hold him in contempt for his association with the king.

There's no denying the way my heartbeat quickened when I first saw him earlier today. Or my excitement at finding him near the docks.

Both are signs of attraction. So I know better than to be standing here on the dock, trading barbs with him. And yet . . .

"What are you doing here?" I ask again. It's been many years since the king sent men to Murwood End, and though we trade often with both Meria and Edingham, its nobles rarely visit our shores. Except for one reason.

"I am not at liberty to discuss it."

He acts exactly as I'd expect a member of the Curia would.

No, not just any member. A commander. Skilled in battle, loyal to the king, not a man to be trifled with. But I've never been one to follow rules.

"Not at liberty?" I freeze when he takes a step toward me.

Aware of the looks we're getting, I hold my ground. Although most of the Voyagers wear mail hauberk and chausses as he does, his brightly colored tunic, emblazoned with the Merian coat of arms, clearly marks him a Southerner. Fine fabrics for a fine lord.

"I make you nervous?"

Oddly, no.

I shake my head. "Curious"—for more reasons than I'm willing to name—"but not nervous."

That seems to surprise him.

"I've not met a maid like you before, Aedre."

"There you are," a familiar voice says as footsteps hustle toward us.

Damnation. Not now. Not him.

"Your father bid me find you."

Agnar sidesteps a fisherman passing in the opposite direction, his gaze never leaving the commander. I've no more desire to introduce the two than I do to leave and return to the forge and inform my father about this discussion.

But I need to.

Nothing occurs in Murwood End in secret. From nobles and captains to freemen and fishermen, all will know of this conversation between the king's man and me.

"My father can wait," I inform Agnar, who looks at me as if he's tempted to snatch me away at this very moment. Eyeing the commander suspiciously, he introduces himself.

"Agnar Haroldson."

Lord d'Abella does not flinch at the clipped introduction.

"Lord Vanni d'Abella."

I roll my eyes at their display, unable to say which of them puffs their chest out more than the other. Agnar, despite my having told him many times over the years we are more akin to brother and sister than husband and wife, asks for my hand often. Thankfully, it's been some time, however, and he's been lately spotted with the miller's daughter.

It would be a good match. Both of them are kindhearted and pleasant to look at, and their children would come into the world blessed in many ways. If they marry, I will be happy for them.

But at the moment, Agnar is not thinking of the miller's daughter. He glares at the Southerner as I did earlier. Though why I should feel compelled to defend the man, I do not know. And yet I find myself saying, "He is Curia Commander to King Galfrid."

We know little of southern politics here—our trade with them is sparser than our dealings with the islands to the north—but we know the history of Meria. Of its structures, of its past. We know what led Murwood End to isolate itself by more than just geography.

And although there's no love lost for the king, there's no denying "commander" is a coveted title. This lord's position changes everything. Agnar, a warrior himself, visibly changes at the news, straightening and losing some of his aggression.

"First commander, or second?" he asks, cocking his head. "Or are you the Knight Commander?"

All signal greatness. A king's second is a skilled knight, indeed, and the Knight's Commander leads the king's men into battle. But the first commander is regarded as the one person in the kingdom most capable of keeping the king, and his people, safe.

"First commander."

The way he says it sends a chill down my back. When Lord d'Abella looks at me, I know for certain he exposes my weakness as a Garra.

A love healer who's never desired a man so deeply that naught else mattered. My grandmother always insisted I'd feel that way myself someday, and I finally do.

For the wrong man.

"Your men are within the Sailor's Inn?" Agnar asks.

"Aye."

"I've just left there. They said you are looking for Master Aldwine?"

Lord d'Abella glances at me.

Agnar's words have shaken me to my core, but I don't let it show.

"Go on," I say, finding it easy to sound annoyed. "Agnar is a man. Certainly you are at liberty to tell him what you could not tell me." Then I spin on my heel and walk away.

The commander calls for me to return, but I make my way along the docks, watching as a ship glides toward shore. Walking by villagers who bid a good day to me, and I them, I slip unseen between two stone buildings. One of them, I realize, is the inn where Lord d'Abella's men reside, and I pull up my hood as a barrier against watchful eyes as I watch the ship grow larger.

Is it Kipp's boat?

I pray it is not.

Stay away. They've come for you again.

As the ship veers closer, I see it is not his, which means my friend is still safely out to sea. But he will return soon.

And there can be only one reason the king's men are here for him.

CHAPTER FIVE
AEDRE

"Take this." I shove a coin into the boy's hand. "Give the smith a message."

The boy's eyes widen as he stares at the coin. This prompts me to give him another, knowing he sees too few of them in those small hands. "I am Aedre, his daughter." A fact that he likely already knows. "Tell him I've been delayed but will return before sunset. Can you do that?"

He nods vigorously and runs away. I will still receive a blistering from Father, but at least he will not worry for my safety. Pulling the hood down a bit farther, I enter and look for them.

There.

Thankfully, their leader does not appear to have found his way back to them yet. Ordering a tankard of ale, I sit as close as possible with my back to two of the men. Courtesy of his wife, Sailor's Inn is always well kept, if muddy near the doors on rainy days. Boards serve as tables, and high-backed settles and stools are scattered all around. Behind the long board where some sit to drink, shelves full of pewter dishes and earthenware mugs are stacked nearly to overflowing. On cool days, the stone hearth in the corner is lit, always surprising those who come from the south, unused to our cold, rainy days, even in the summer.

The others do not pay me any notice, and with luck, none of the Sailor's Inn patrons will either. It is not at all unusual for a woman to frequent the dockside tavern alone. Though I suspect, from my understanding and from Lord d'Abella's reaction earlier, it would be odd indeed in the south.

It doesn't take long for them to speak of their objective. I've positioned myself in such a way that they're all seated behind me. My view is of the innkeeper and his attendants, plus all manner of patrons, but I need not see the Southerners to hear them clearly.

"Will we stay?"

"His instructions were clear. We don't return without him."

Him. Kipp.

"Where do you think Vanni has gone?" the first man asked.

"Getting the townspeople to adore him, most likely."

That was said with reverence, not malice. So people like this commander? And his men respect him?

"Will it matter if we cannot gain access to the man?"

A grunt greets his question. "It did surprise me to learn he's so infrequently home."

The remoteness of Kipp's manor and infrequency of his visits ashore are well-known here but apparently less so to the men who would persuade him to return to his birthplace.

His instructions were clear. We don't return without him.

Why has the king sent for him after all these years? Especially since Kipp made it very clear the last time they came he would never, ever return south.

"There he is."

I spin around without thinking and then turn back in my

seat quickly. Of course they're talking of their commander and not of Kipp.

Did he notice me?

"Have you learned anything?" one of his men ask.

I can hear a shuffling sound as Lord d'Abella takes a seat, blissfully unaware of my presence. Thank the heavens.

"Only that the women of Murwood End are curious indeed."

I'd not planned on drinking the ale, having merely ordered it to avoid suspicion. But I take a long sip, shaken by his presence. By his words.

"Curious how?"

"Does it matter? We're here to find . . ."

One of the men, the commander maybe, clears his throat.

"They are much too forward for my liking," d'Abella continues. An odd silence descends over the group, broken by him. "I met one in particular, the blacksmith's daughter, who seems to have strange notions about the role women should play. As if they are equal to us men."

The group laughs, and although it's exactly the kind of remark that would normally move me to anger, I'm disappointed instead. Despite the look he gave the ship captain, I'd hoped he would not be one of those men who see women as nothing more than property. Even here, in Murwood, there are those who are still influenced by Southern ideas. After all, Murwood End was originally founded by former Southerners.

"Mayhap she believes such things because she is not comely."

I nearly choke on my ale.

"Nay," the coxcomb says, "she is quite comely. More comely, in fact, than any woman I've met before."

Stupid heart, that it would beat so erratically for a man

such as this. If I thought his arrogance was bad, his thoughts on women are even worse.

"'Tis a fact?"

Again, silence. He does not answer. I resist the urge to spin in my seat, knowing Lord d'Abella is facing me. But I look forward to telling Kipp, when he does return, to sail back out at once and never speak to the king's men, who want only to use him, I'm sure, for their own nefarious purposes.

"Aye, 'tis very much a fact."

I do look up then, for the words are whispered into my ear. I did not even hear him approaching. My shoulders rise and fall in . . . anger? Nay. Excitement. I'm disgusted by the knowledge, but there's no denying it.

"How long have you known I was here?"

The commander sits across the table from me, ale in hand. Did he say those things for my benefit? Knowing I was here? Or do I only wish it to be so?

"Since the moment I came inside."

His gaze is much too intense.

"Because you are trained to notice threats to you and your men?"

He takes a swig of ale, slow to answer.

"Nay. Because a woman such as you could not escape my notice, even with a hood covering her head."

I hate that his words affect me so.

Taking down the hood, I sip my ale to afford myself a moment to think.

"Strange notions indeed," I mutter.

I am wholly unprepared for Lord d'Abella's smile. Faint lines form around his amused eyes, and I know for certain he did say those words for my benefit.

I repeat his man's words. "Mayhap she believes such things because she is not comely."

"I informed my men we had a companion," he says with a smile. "And they caught on quickly."

So it was all a ruse.

"Do you enjoy sporting with women so, Lord d'Abella?"

In answer, he leans back, crossing his legs in front of him.

"As I said Aedre, 'tis not our way to insult strangers, and I cannot answer that question without causing offense to you."

He could say my name over and over and over again, and I'd not tire of hearing it.

"So 'tis true," I say. "You are a cruel man, indeed."

His smile remains.

"I do enjoy sporting with women. As they enjoy sporting with me. But surely you would not decry finding pleasure in the act. As a Garra."

He drinks, clearly pleased with himself. His men are likely listening to every word we speak, so I do not indulge him. My thoughts on the pleasure between a man and a woman are mine alone.

Although I do have thoughts, and plenty of them, on the matter.

"I did not mean sporting of a sexual nature, as you well know."

"My apologies, my lady. I am a sexual creature and find such thoughts too often occupy me. Perhaps you can help me find a cure?"

While I *could* offer such help, and have done so before as a Garra, I do not for one moment believe he is doing anything other than . . .

Sporting?

Teasing?

Oh dear. Truly it does not matter. I did not come here to flirt with the man but to learn more of his intentions toward Kipp.

"I could, but will not."

"Mmm. 'Tis a shame. Perhaps I could be persuaded to tell you more of our mission here if you were to allow me to retain your services."

My mouth forms into a wide O, my jaw nearly dropping to the ground.

"You would not?"

I say it even though I very much believe he would hold his purpose here hostage.

"Aye," he says. "I would."

My mind works quickly. As much as I would like to gain access to his information, I could never agree to such an outrageous proposal.

First, he has no actual ailment, only a contrived one.

Second, my father would never agree to it.

Third, his intentions are not clear to me.

"Why do you make such an offer?"

Is he a lecher after all? I do not believe so, but what other reason could he have? The commander has no way of knowing I am aware of the circumstances of Kipp's birth. Few people are aware the king has a bastard son, although he has clearly informed his Curia. If the commander is not using me to gain access to Kipp, why does he want me to treat an ailment he does not possess?

"You intrigue me," he says.

I watch for signs of ill intent. Of dishonesty.

But he does not look away. Nor does he use his hands overly much after saying those words that set my heart to racing. His voice is strong, his eyes equally so.

"I do not like you." While not a lie, it is also not precisely the truth.

"Perhaps one of the reasons I am intrigued," he says, his lips tipping up.

"Nor do I believe you need treatment."

"There is but one way for you to find out."

Father will kill me.

"My fee is high."

"I will pay it."

"Why?" I ask again.

The commander leans forward, putting his ale on the table between us. "You looked me in the eyes the moment we met."

True enough. Then again, I do not believe it is a sin to do so. Despite what the church teaches, the mere act of looking directly into a man's eyes cannot tempt him into sin. And if it *were* possible, it would be a mark of the man's weak character.

"And I do so now," I prod.

"Indeed."

I can hear my very heartbeat in my ears as we look at each other. In the end, there is but one answer.

I need to find out more information for Kipp.

Or so I tell myself.

"I will do it. But you must tell me why you are here."

His men grow silent, proof that they've been listening to our conversation despite their chatter.

"I'll answer one of your questions each time we meet," he offers.

"About your reasons for being in Murwood End?"

"Aye. One each visit."

I empty my ale, stand, and say, "Very well. Then we shall meet here tomorrow at this time."

The bargain is one that favors me. Vanni d'Abella will get nothing from it he does not already have. So why do I feel like I'm about to lose everything?

CHAPTER SIX

VANNI

"*T*is a foolish plan."

The others have retired to the private quarters provided by the innkeeper. Only Sir Thomas and I remain in the common room, though I'm beginning to regret the decision to stay for one more ale.

"You've a better one?"

As the night wears on, the crowd decidedly more bawdy than before, I ignore the urge to engage with those who watch us. If we're to stay in Murwood End to await Master Aldwine's return, we must not engage in battle with the people here. But one man in particular, who's been watching us all eve, his jaw tight with aggression, makes my fingers twitch.

"Than seeking treatment by a Garra for a made-up condition so you can gain information that will give us access to the boy? Aye. We intercept him on his return."

There was no mention of her being a Garra, but if this is the same woman rumored to be as a sister to Aldwine, I may gain more than just information. But I could be wrong and will keep the thought to myself.

Thomas, a good friend in addition to his role as Knight Commander in the Curia, raises his hand to the maid, whom we've learned is the innkeeper's daughter. Comely, perhaps having seen twenty or so summers, she appears, like most women, to have fallen for Thomas's charms.

"Ale, my lord?"

"He is the only lord here, mistress. I am but a humble servant of the king."

"Humble servant indeed," I mutter. The irony is not lost on me. He may be pressing me about Aedre, but he's a merciless flirt.

The maid smiles coyly at Thomas as she walks away.

"Careful, Thomas," I say. "If we're to stay here, you'd do well not to dip your oar in that water."

"Says the man who's meeting the Garra for no good reason."

True enough.

"Does she so freely practice here without repercussion?" he asks.

"Apparently."

Thomas's maid returns with his ale, and while he speaks with her, I think of Aedre. Did she agree to meet me simply for coin? Or did I detect a hint of attraction from her?

"I don't like it." Thomas, finished with the maid, leans forward. "Hinton will be gathering support even now. And yet we sit here, idle, doing naught about it."

"Naught but securing the one man who can challenge his claim."

I wave my hand, ignoring my drunken foe, who's looking at me even now.

"This is the most important battleground, Thomas. If we leave here without him . . ."

I drink to avoid finishing that thought. If we leave here without him, Meria is doomed to be ruled by a cruel and inept king. A man who cares for naught but securing the power his father, the king's brother, was never able to claim. Of course, King Galfrid could name another heir. Some distant kin with tenuous ties to the royal family. But Hinton has a silver tongue that belies his base nature. Some men care more for advancing their own positions than they do for the good of the realm. And those men will be easily swayed by his lofty promises. He will rule unlike any of the kings of Meria before him, and all will be worse off for it.

It is true none know firsthand the true measure of Kipp Aldwine, but from reports Galfrid has gathered throughout the years, we know he is both strong and honorable. A man unlike Hinton.

"To think Edingham was our biggest threat mere months ago," I muse. Now, those skirmishes along the border seem inconsequential compared to the chaos our kingdom will endure if this mission fails.

"If the boy refuses to come, Hinton cannot be the answer."

Though he speaks the words softly, I shake my head. This is not the place to discuss such matters as a vision of Matteo, the man who should have been king, flashes before me.

Once again, I feel the strange pang of knowing I could have been on that boat.

Pushing the thoughts back down, I say, "He is no boy. Master Aldwine has seen more than thirty summers."

Galfrid still speaks of him as the babe he sent away those many years ago, but Kipp Aldwine is a strong, capable man. From what we've heard in the south, he's reputedly the fiercest of all Voyagers.

"Also not a boy? Your opponent this evening."

I'm not surprised Thomas has taken notice of the man as well. And he's right to do so. If we are to stay in Murwood End, the vitriol he's sending our way, stares that are becoming harder to ignore, cannot be tolerated. It will only encourage bad behavior.

"Shall I get the others?"

"Nay."

I stand.

"Christ's body," Thomas mutters behind me.

Unwilling to spill blood in the very place we're taking shelter, I break eye contact with the man and stride out the door. The smell of sea air, more crisp than in the south, welcomes me. The docks are dark, quiet, and largely empty, though the moon provides enough light for me to see my adversary as he strides out the door after me.

"Southerner." He spits on the ground in front of me.

"A king's man," one of his companions warns, as if to dissuade him. At least one of the local men has some wits about him.

"The king's commander," Thomas informs them both. If he intended for the words to caution the man, they seem to have the opposite effect. He unsheathes his sword.

I sigh. Loudly.

"We have no king here." He spits again and advances, barely waiting for me to unsheathe my own weapon before raising his against me.

If I were not so weary from travel, I might have enjoyed a bit of sport. But this has been a long day, one I'm ready to end.

So instead of engaging with him, I simply wait for his thrust. When it comes, I rebuff it, knocking his sword from his hand after just three attempts. Not an easy feat given his size and strength, but unlike my opponent, my intent was not to harm or maim.

Sword tip pointed to his neck, I back away, addressing the small crowd that has gathered.

"I am Lord Vanni d'Abella, Curia Commander to King

Galfrid. Aye, a Southerner. But I've no fight with you. Our purpose here is a peaceful one."

I pull away, sheathing my sword, and reach for my opponent's hand.

And wait.

Finally, to a round of cheers, he shakes it. Thomas hands the man his sword.

"I have no fight with you," I repeat.

He responds by snatching his sword and thanking Thomas with a scowl. But my purpose has been served. Although not as fruitful as I would have liked, the day was hardly a disaster.

"Come. 'Tis time to find our beds."

Thomas follows me back into the inn's small hall, and I take a deep, calming breath, giving silent thanks no blood was shed this night.

CHAPTER SEVEN

AEDRE

"*A*mma!" I sit up in my bed, surprised to see her in my chamber so early. My grandmother has never been an early riser.

"Good morn, my child."

Though she uses the term each day, I smile every time. Opening the shutters, she moves toward my bed and sits. Amma moves more slowly of late, and it worries me.

"You spoke to your father last eve?"

Though our manor house is no castle, it is large enough to provide ample room for my father and me, my grandmother, and one maidservant. It is a comfortable home, the only one I've known.

"Aye."

It was not a pleasant conversation, especially since I had to tell him I'd not be at the forge today. Balancing apprenticing for him and training with Amma has been a lifelong struggle, and one that I very much long to end.

"He was not happy, but I secured two bushels of grain from Lord Bailor for easing his joints, so Father was much appeased."

"You kept the mixture in the pot until 'twas deep red?"

I throw off the coverlet and rise from the bed.

"Aye, Amma. And used hallowleek as well."

"Oh?"

Plump, grey-haired, and always smiling, Amma is the most beautiful woman in the world to me. I look at her now as she waits for me to answer. For a moment, I'm overcome with a feeling of abundance. She's so much more than a grandmother to me—she's a friend and adviser. A teacher. What would I do without her?

Such silly thoughts this morn. Though no sillier than those I had as I laid my head down to sleep. The dark-haired commander refused to go away, even in my dreams.

I make my way to the basin on the table and pick up the cloth that sits beside it. "Do you remember the book Agnar brought back from his last voyage? From the healer in Stoughrock who told him of the hallowleek?"

Amma nods. "I remember."

"I believe it worked, but will check on Lord Bailor today."

"Agnar is in love with you, Aedre."

My hand freezes over the bowl of lavender-scented water.

"Nay. He is but a friend."

"Aedre?"

"Very well," I admit. "Still, he is but a friend." I resume my ministrations, running the wet cloth along my forearm.

"Your father is becoming impatient."

I know it well.

"I've seen just twenty-five summers. Not an old maid . . ."

"But neither a youngin."

Finished, I slip on a new shift.

"I will marry for love or not at all."

Amma knows this, so I wonder what has prompted this discussion.

"He blames me for that sentiment."

I hate when she frowns so. It doesn't fit her usual disposition.

"And yet, he loves you well."

Father may wish Amma weren't training me to be a Garra, a title given only to those with both the blood and training, but he loves us both. Just as he did my mother.

A Garra would never marry a man without love, for she knows the consequences all too well.

"Hmph. So tell me of the commander."

Wincing, I open my trunk and stare at the gowns stored within it.

"Aedre?"

Pulling out a simple one of deep blue, I close the trunk and shake out the fabric, laying it across the top. A breeze from the open window blows a strand of hair onto my face. Brushing it away, I sit in the wooden chair opposite my grandmother.

"So you already heard about him," I ask.

Amma knows everything that happens in Murwood End, perhaps even more so than Father. Though I planned to tell her about Lord d'Abella, I wanted to gather my wits about me first.

"You spoke with him?" she presses.

"I did. He shared little of his purpose for being here, so I snuck into Sailor's Inn and listened to his men. Overheard them speaking of Kipp."

Amma's eyes widen.

"Of Kipp?"

She is as protective of him as I am. When Kipp's mother was cast out of Castle d'Almerita with him, the king's babe, she made her way here, to Murwood End. My amma and Kipp's mother grew very close. Eventually, she married the mercenary who'd accompanied her here. I saw less of Kipp in those years as he traveled often with his father, but his mother fell ill and died. Our shared pain over being mother-less brought us closer again.

"Aye. They said, 'His instructions were clear. We don't return without him.'"

My grandmother crosses herself. She is not an overly religious woman, preferring the teachings of her ancestors to the church's increasingly zealous guidance. The Shadow Warriors, men who fight for the church, are as feared here in Murwood as they are in the south. At times they've been used against both kingdoms when the church disagrees with their edicts. Other times, they fight for the people. Some see them as a force of good against evil, but others dislike their blind devotion to the Prima.

"Why does the king send for him?"

"I do not know but aim to find out. The commander caught me listening to his men, teased me for it, and said he could use a Garra to treat his overly amorous ways. So"—I forge ahead—"I agreed to it. I'm to meet with him this afternoon."

I hold my breath, waiting for her response.

"Does he truly suffer from such an affliction?"

My heart races at the question. At the thought of meeting him again.

"Nay."

"What is his intention with you?"

Warmth floods my cheeks.

"He is attracted to you."

"I believe so."

Father would forbid such a dangerous arrangement. The very idea of spending time with a man who thinks of me in that way, especially one who has shown a clear disdain for capable women . . .

But it is a risk I will gladly take, for Kipp.

And because you're attracted to him too, insists a traitorous voice in my head.

"You will meet in a crowded place."

"Of course."

"Noblemen cannot be trusted, my child, whether they be from the south or the east. You know what you are."

"I know it well."

The lessons of our ancestors, one of whom was killed by such a lord for her skills, linger. That we should be so feared for remedies that can be found within nature, within ourselves, once confused me. But no longer. I see now that as Garra learn, and become stronger, they begin to transcend what can be explained in the natural world alone.

"Most especially a Curia commander. But you must go."

"Aye," I agree, "I must."

She stands, with some struggle. I leap forward to help, but she shoves my hand away. Amma will not allow any to coddle her, even me.

"Kipp could return at any time. We must learn why the king has sent for him," she says.

"He will not go with them."

"No." She appears thoughtful. "He will not. But Kipp will be better prepared if we learn their purpose. 'Tis been many years since the king has attempted to claim him."

So why now? Does it have anything to do with the latest disputes at the border?

"Be careful, my child. If I were stronger, I'd accompany you."

I hate that Amma rarely leaves the manor. These days, her longest walks are to the forge. Distances and stairs pose difficulties for her.

"I will be well," I assure her, tying a gold-threaded rope belt around my waist. "He is kind enough, for a nobleman."

Amma lifts her chin. "Do not mistake cunning for kindness."

"Of course."

"And I will deal with your father."

I wrap my arms around her, breathing in the scent that is uniquely my grandmother. "Thank you, Amma."

She lets go.

"Be well, child." She looks into my eyes. "I do not like this. Not at all."

Amma's instincts are never wrong. Her words send a chill through me, but I end our conversation by saying, "But all is well in Murwood."

I've grown up with that expression, used to end all conversations about happenings in the two kingdoms we distance ourselves from.

"All is well in Murwood," she repeats.

But her expression belies her words.

CHAPTER EIGHT
VANNI

"*H*ow are the men?"

Thomas winks at a maid, who smiles back at him as she passes us. Another day, another maid for Thomas to flirt with. Standing at the front of the inn, waiting for Aedre, my companion attracts more attention than I would wish.

"Going mad," he answers.

We've been in Murwood End for one full day. I'm restless and imagine the others feel the same way. While they spent the day ingratiating themselves to the locals, I met with two of Murwood's lords to assure them our visit is an unofficial one.

Unofficial for their purposes, at least.

For Kipp Aldwine, it is very official. We are here to offer him the crown. Prepared to give him anything he desires to convince him to come south.

"Did Lord Bailor press you on our purpose?"

Another woman, another wink. The man is incorrigible.

"Aye." I consider my meeting with him that morning. "A bit, but I pacified him, I believe."

"You didn't mention the boy's name?"

I'm unsure why Thomas insists on referring to a man older than him as a boy.

"Of course not."

"There she is."

At his words, I push away from the wall and stand tall. Which, of course, prompts a fit of laughter from Thomas.

"*You* chastise *me* for flirting?"

Hitting him, prompting an "ow," I watch as the Garra approaches.

So serious. Her full lips are pursed together, brows furrowed. She does not smile easily, that I can tell. Even so, her beauty dulls even the bright blue sky framing her from behind. Dressed simply but elegantly, she glides toward me, greeting those around her with a simple nod.

"She's beautiful, that I'll allow."

Ignoring Thomas, I prepare to greet her. Prepare to spar with her.

For there's no doubt she doesn't like me. An affliction to which I'm unaccustomed.

"Good day," she greets us.

Lavender overpowers the scent of salt air.

"Good day, my lady," Thomas says smoothly, bowing.

Her response is polite but cool. At least she appears to like Thomas as little as she does me. I can't help but grin at his stricken expression.

"Shall we?" I move toward the door.

"Nay, not in there." She gestures for me to follow her, her expression brooking no refusal. Thomas and I exchange a look, but she's already walking. I bid him farewell, and the last thing I see before I hurry after her is Thomas winking.

The Garra walks from the inn toward the docks. No ships are in port, but the area still bustles with activity. A fishing village never sleeps, and this one is no different.

"Where are we going?" I ask as the docks end.

"Away from prying eyes and overly curious ears."

It's clear we're following a path, and with my attention on our surroundings—timber-framed buildings with thatched roofs, others built of stone—I don't notice when she veers off in another direction. But *she* certainly notices.

"Nay! This way."

I stop and strain to see what's ahead.

"Why don't you wish to continue this way?" I ask.

She grimaces.

"I shall go ahead and see for myself."

Aedre exhales loudly, frustrated. "That way lies the forge where my father works."

Ah yes, she's the blacksmith's daughter.

"He would not be keen to see us together?"

Understandable, as Aedre is an unmarried maid.

"Even less if he knew the reason. This way."

Following her through the winding paths between buildings, I consider her words. So her father does not care for her chosen profession. Interesting. Back home, without a father's approval, she would find it difficult to pursue such a path.

A dog emerges from what appears to be the tailor's shop. Stopping, I reach down to pet him without thinking. It's attention he wants, and I'm more than willing to give it.

"Good day, Lady Aedre."

The tailor.

"And . . ."

I stand, offering my hand. "Lord d'Abella, at your service."

Though quite old and unable to stand completely straight, he shakes my hand vigorously. "Ronald, my lord."

I step back, aware Aedre wishes to move on. "Good day, Ronald. To you and . . . ?"

"Dog."

Did I hear him correctly? "Your dog's name is Dog?"

"Aye, my lord."

I try not to smile. "Very good. 'Twas my pleasure to meet you both."

As we move away, I notice something quite surprising.

"You're smiling," I say to Aedre without thinking. But the smile disappears as soon as I mention it, my words snuffing it out of existence.

"This way," she says with an aggrieved sniff.

Emerging once again at the water's edge, the docks giving way to a rocky coastline, we continue to walk. As the buildings fall away, I watch her. Curious.

"Should we not stay in the village?"

No answer.

"You do not know me. What if I . . ."

She stops, moving so quickly I'm not in the least prepared for the knife she points at my neck. Where did it even come from? I shove away a vision of it tucked between her breasts.

Curia Commander indeed.

Eyes blazing, she doesn't move her hand away. The tip of her blade is so close I can feel its presence just above my skin.

"Once again, you underestimate a woman's place."

Definitely lavender. I can smell it easily. Although my well-being should be foremost in my thoughts right now, it's not.

"I vow not to do so again."

From the look in her eyes, it's obvious she doesn't believe my claim, but it's true. We are at an impasse, one I have to end.

"Shall we begin our training now? You are a Garra. Tell me, Aedre, what am I thinking?"

I'm thinking of two round breasts nearly pressed against me. I'm thinking of her sweet scent and the small smile I spied back in the village. I'm thinking this woman is unlike any other.

Something flashes in her eyes. "Do not . . ."

Too late.

"You are quite beautiful."

She lowers her hand, but I grasp it before she moves away.

"What am I thinking?" he presses.

"I'm not sure what tall tales you've heard, my lord, but I do not read thoughts."

Her wrist is so small, so delicate in my hand. Very much unlike her personality. Delicate is not a word I'd use to describe her. Not at all.

"But you do read expressions? Feelings?"

She snatches her hand back. "I do."

"And?"

She makes a most unladylike sound. "And yours says you'd like to stick your cock in me. What of it?"

She continues on, forcing me to take long strides to catch her.

"Nay, Lady Aedre."

We reach an outcropping of rocks and, weaving her way through it, Aedre climbs deftly toward one particularly flat stone. She arranges her skirts and sits, and I settle in beside her. Though it is large enough for both of us, we sit closer than we might have elsewhere.

The sound of the surf and seagulls reminds me of home, and the spot is as beautiful as the woman beside me.

To our right lies the village, a circle of buildings with the road we took to reach it from the south clearly visible. And in front of us, my favorite of all, the sea. Not a turquoise blue like back home, but an angry grey-blue—defiant, like the people of Murwood. Like the woman sitting next to me.

Much too close.

"I'd not stick my cock in you, if given the chance."

Her brows rise. "Then I am not the Garra my grand-mother thinks I am."

She misunderstands me.

"Oh, you do not misread my thoughts, Aedre. I've thought of it, aye. I've wondered if you might smile if I kissed you. I fell asleep last eve imagining myself making love to you."

If I said as much to any woman at court, my cheek would have already been properly slapped. Then again, not one of them would accuse me on our second meeting of wanting to *stick my cock* in them.

"Which brings us to your affliction." We both know I have none, but she says it with confidence. "Do you find yourself entertaining such thoughts every time you meet a woman you desire?"

"Nay, I do not."

"Tell me, Lord—"

"Vanni."

"Tell me, Vanni, why you've secured my services."

Leaning back against my hands, I consider her question.

"You are preparing to lie to me," she accuses.

Something about Aedre's very casual position, legs crossed under her skirts, so at odds with the daggers she shoots from her eyes, makes me smile.

"'Tis not amusing."

"I'm not laughing at your words."

There's no denying her guess was somewhat accurate. I do not mean to lie to her, precisely, but the version of the truth I provide will be a tailored one, intended to help me gain information.

"Then you are laughing at me?"

"Are you always so combative?" I gesture out to sea, to the

blue sky beyond. "'Tis a glorious day. Is this such a bad way to earn coin?"

No answer.

"Why do you dislike me so?"

That she answers easily.

"I do not know your purpose, and like most Southerners, you have antiquated notions of women. And . . ." She pauses.

"And? 'Tis not enough?"

Apparently not. I can feel myself smirking.

"I dislike nobles. Most especially your kind."

"If I came from the court of Edingham, would that make a difference?"

She pulls her skirts in tighter against her crossed legs. "Nay."

Small relief.

"You resent that I'm a king's man," I guess.

She nods. "Surely you know my ancestors have not been treated kindly by either court."

"Many years ago, perhaps. But there is no longer much public antipathy toward the Garra. Well," I qualify, "except by some in the church."

She looks at me as if I were a boy of five.

"That does not equate to kind treatment. Are Garra openly welcomed in d'Almerita? Are they given the opportunity to practice? Or are they relegated to the outskirts of town, allowed to exist only if they follow Merian customs, and only then if 'tis deemed appropriate?"

"I know of no Garra in d'Almerita, but they would be accepted there."

Her expression is beyond incredulous.

"The king is a good man who cares for his people," I continue.

"He is a fool."

At least her vitriol extends beyond me. I will not argue

her point, not even for Galfrid, but I cannot allow our conversation to continue on in this vein.

"My purpose," I say, changing topics, "is to learn what I can of Master Aldwine in order to sway him to our cause."

I can tell she's taken aback by my candidness. Which I hadn't been prepared to offer. But whether it's her profession or her nature that makes it so, Aedre is unnaturally astute. Half measures will not do with her.

"Which is?"

"One question each day," I remind her.

"But I've asked none."

She does not flinch. Recalling her words, I realize she is correct.

I do not know your purpose here. Tell me, Vanni, why you've secured my services.

"You are clever, indeed. Go ahead then, ask it."

"What cause sends you to Murwood End to speak with Master Aldwine?"

She does know him.

I see the truth of it in her eyes. Too eager for an answer that has little to do with her. The question now is, how well? Is she the woman with whom he's been linked?

Are they . . .

Something tightens inside me, and I ask, "How do you know him?"

"You first."

Though I cannot tell her the entire truth, some of it will suffice.

"I've a message from the king for him."

Unsatisfied with my answer, she's about to ask another question when I stop her.

"One each day. Now tell me how you know him."

Even I can hear that my voice is too tight.

"I mean to say, 'tis clear you know the man. Will you tell me how?"

She lifts her chin and smiles, although this isn't at all the smile I'd hoped for. There's something secretive about it. Triumphant. "We were raised together," she says, "here in Murwood."

Which is an interesting answer, but she gave me precisely nothing useful.

"You asked why I've secured your services." I breathe in the crisp sea air.

"And you answered already. To gain information."

I sit up and cross my legs to match her manner of sitting.

"Aye, but also for my other affliction."

"So you are overly amorous? Or are your affections just not returned? Because that is a very different sort of problem."

I choose to laugh rather than be insulted. "Nay. You accused me of having antiquated notions of women. And indeed, I know of none at court who sit the way you do in public, so casually, or accuse me of wanting to stick my cock in them."

A cock that I've been attempting to tame since the moment I spied her outside the inn. Everything about Aedre—her long, loose hair, her thoughtful eyes and full mouth, the intensity of her expressions, her quick wit. Everything about her entices me.

"You will instruct me of your women. Your ways."

"Will I?"

I take out a coin purse and hand it to her. Fool that I am, I'm grateful for the excuse to touch her.

"Can you resist such an offer?"

Can you resist me?

"I could," she says confidently. "It serves my purpose not to."

"Hmm. And what purpose is that?"

When she stands, I realize the sun is beginning to set. Have we been out here so long already?

"Mayhap I will tell you on the morrow." She puts the coin purse in a pocket sewn into her gown. Likely the same pocket where her knife resides. "Or mayhap not."

CHAPTER NINE
AEDRE

*S*moke rises from the forge, the smell of coal dust and molten iron oddly comforting. I walk inside, grab an apron, and begin to work. Father doesn't pause as he hammers away, the clanging sound of hammer meeting iron ringing in my ears.

I look at his work.

A sword, and a fine one at that.

Amery, my father's apprentice, nods in greeting. Though he's not seen twenty summers, he's a fine apprentice and will make a master smith someday.

I pick up a set of metal spoons in obvious need of filing and begin to smooth the sharp edges. Though part of me wishes my father was between pieces, as we need to talk, the other part of me is glad for the respite, as it will be an uncomfortable conversation.

Amma waited for me last eve, as she typically retires early, to tell me that Father had gone to Hester's Tavern. As it was his second visit in a matter of days, Amma is convinced he has feelings for the alewife. I disagree. He's visited the tavern more oft of late, there's no denying that, but not once in all my years has Father shown interest in another woman. I would welcome it, of course. But when my mother died giving birth to me, he swore, according to Amma, he'd not take another woman to his bed or as his wife.

And he never had.

Despite both Amma and I encouraging him otherwise.

"Daydreaming will not get those spoons filed."

Despite Father's gruff tone, I turn and wrinkle my nose at him. I've done this since I was a babe, according to him, and he cannot resist it.

"Come."

Wiping his hand on an already dirty apron, he strides from the dark room into the bright light of the day. The docks are visible from here, the sea beyond them rough this morning.

Picking up a jug of water from the ground, he pours it into a leather skin. Father leans against the side of the stone shop and drinks deeply.

"'Tis a fine weapon you were forging," I say, wiping my hands instinctively on my apron before I register they aren't yet dirty.

"A commission from the new lad."

Everyone is a "lad" to my father. If King Galfrid himself had seen one less summer than him, Father would call him lad as well.

"Which one?"

If there is a sword to be forged, Father will prioritize it above all else. As the only smith in Murwood, his days are usually spent making tools and nails.

"The commander."

Vanni commissioned a weapon from my father?

"When did he speak to you?"

And why did he not mention it to me? After we parted

ways last eve, I told Amma about our conversation. As was her custom, she did not tread lightly with her advice.

"Your attraction to him will cause poor judgment."

Not that I *told* her of any such attraction, but she is a Garra, after all.

"This morn, at daybreak."

Oh, he is a slippery one.

"What did you think of him?"

Father takes another swig of water before putting the skin back down. He will not bring it inside the forge, even sealed. Coal dust tends to find its way inside of every crevice in the shop.

"He is Galfrid's man."

Apparently that was all he planned to say. It should have been enough. None in Murwood have any great love for either court, their appeals to our people to fight for one side or the other something we do not tolerate.

"Aye, he is that."

"What of you?"

Father knows I spoke to him that first day, but unless Amma decided to tell him, he doesn't know about our private meetings. I plan to save the coin and give it to Father when the commander is well on his way back to the southern coast.

"He is not to be trusted," Father adds, which I know to be true.

Lying to my father does not come naturally to me. So I find myself saying, "They are looking for Kipp."

Our eyes meet.

"I've heard the same," he says. "We need to warn him."

Father knows of his true parentage, of course, after Kipp's mother told us all so many years ago.

"Aye," I agree. "Do you think he will return soon?"

Father nodded. "Any day. You can keep watch for him.

51

You spend as much time wandering the village as you do in the forge."

What good luck that he should suggest it.

"I know you do not approve . . ."

Father pushes himself away from the wall. His face is an entreaty. "I would keep you safe above all, Aedre."

He glances over my shoulder, and his expression changes so drastically my stomach drops. I follow his gaze and groan.

Father Beald.

I'd not heard the Elderman was in town.

Traveling from port to port, he lands at the docks in Murwood End twice or thrice a year.

His visits are much the same each time. Around the village he goes, soliciting support for a church to be built right here in Murwood End. He simply cannot understand we need no such structure to believe in many of the same ideals as those who claim the Prima represents God's will here on Earth.

"Good day," my father greets him.

I echo the words, grinding my teeth as I say them.

"Master Dal. Mistress Aedre."

I nod, trying not to let the deliberate slight bother me. Never mind that Garra are given the courtesy title of Lady— he refuses to use it. I care nothing for such trivialities, but I do care about the intentions behind his omission.

He's never been subtle about his scorn for Amma and me, which is the reason my father is unable to contain his distaste for him. I put my hand over Father's, reminding him of the Elderman's power. Even here, in Murwood End, the church can touch us, and Father Beald's visits remind us of the fact.

"Did you come on the Talisman?" my father asks.

"Aye," he answers, regaling us with tales of the bad weather they'd encountered. The Elderman, who despite his title is no older than Father, notices I am not listening and glares at me.

"Working in the smithy today, Mistress Aedre?"

I'm tempted to tell him exactly what I'll be doing this afternoon, but I don't. I've nothing to be ashamed of—I seek only to heal—but Amma often reminds me that he dislikes not only our profession but the Voyagers' unwillingness to build a church, which would allow him, or another, to stay on.

We may worship the same God, but we do not follow the laws of the Prima. To us, he is not God here on Earth but another man, just like Father or Kipp or Agnar. Those views make us a target—that I'm Garra makes the target larger.

If he dislikes us so, mayhap Father Beald should just stay away. Yet he does not, and each time he returns, his threats become more direct.

"Aye, she is assisting me with a new commission. A sword for the king's Curia Commander. You've heard Galfrid's men have come?"

He's diverted the Elderman's attention well.

Father Beald's lips purse, but the extremely verbose Elderman does not answer. So, he knows something.

The Talisman sails from Murwood to the port of Brecklow, north of the Royal Court of Edingham. Surely he could not know why Galfrid's men are here?

"We've heard little of their purpose," I say, as sweetly as I'm able, "but perhaps you know more than we do?"

I do not scare easily, but the look Father Beald gives me isn't one I'd care to see again soon.

"As always, it has been a pleasure speaking with you," he says stiffly. Then he shuffles away, having answered neither of our questions, moving down the winding alleyways toward the center of the village.

My father shakes his head, mutters a word that would

have turned the Elderman's ears red, and turns toward the forge. I follow, prepared to spend my day here before meeting Vanni this afternoon.

If I'm looking forward to that meeting, it is only because I need information. If Father Beald knows something I do not, something that can affect Kipp . . .

Aye, that is the only reason my hands will not steady as I begin filing the spoons again. Although maybe, possibly, it has something to do with the thought of seeing Lord d'Abella again.

CHAPTER TEN
VANNI

"*Ho!* Do we have a man who can best him?"

I hear the taunts and cheers of the men but block them out of my mind. I've one purpose now, and that is to defeat my opponent. Our swords are real, the points sharp. Losing my head today will not do. Thankfully, Galfrid is many miles away.

The king forbids me to take part in such sport, with good reason. Training, with blunted weapons, aye. But this? Nay, he'd not be pleased.

"Ah," someone shouts as a familiar man steps forward. I recognize him as Aedre's friend, a large man who looks part Voyager and part bear. "Agnar has the commander."

Nay, he does not.

The makeshift training yard has filled to capacity. I've been victorious thus far, but my strength is beginning to wane after facing six opponents.

Agnar's sword strikes my shield with a clang that reverberates through my arm. He's strong. And quicker than one would expect for a man his size. Which makes it all the sweeter to close in on victory. Something flashes in his eyes when he realizes he's been backed up against the stone wall of the inn. When he tries to spin his way out, my sword is there. On the other side, a cart laden with grain.

Trapped, he attempts to strike once more, but I am much too close for him to land a good blow. He tosses up his arms, apparently as unwilling as I am to draw blood this day, an easy enough feat with pointed swords.

"Yield," he shouts.

Cheers and groans fill the yard. Though many are disappointed their man has been defeated, I've earned the respect of some.

My goal has been met.

Let Aldwine return to whispers of a king's man who is worthy of his consideration. It wouldn't do much to sway him, but I'll take any advantages I can. I fear we may need them.

"Well fought, Lord d'Abella."

"Vanni," I say. He offers his forearm, and I grasp it gladly. The Voyager sign of respect, and one not easily won. I am exhausted and in need of a bath and a meal before I'm to meet Aedre again.

"Vanni. A name I've not heard before."

As the crowd disperses, my men leave with all the rest. I find myself walking toward the back of the inn with my former opponent.

"They say my mother had a unique . . . way about her," I explain.

"They say?"

We reach the back door of the inn, my temporary home here in Murwood End.

"She died when I was nine. My father too. The sleeping illness took them both."

Agnar looks up to the skies, a gesture of respect for the dead.

Then he glances back at me and says, "I've seen only one man fight as you do."

"Aye, someone from Murwood?"

If there's a man as skilled as I am, he is one I should like to challenge. My abilities were hard won—the result of the brutal lessons the king insisted on from the very day he took me in.

A young boy runs by us, kicking up dirt as he chases a dark brown dog that barks his displeasure at being run down.

"The same one you seek," Agnar says, tilting his head.

All of Murwood knows our purpose for this visit, it seems. Though none can know the reason. Soon enough they'll learn the Oryan has sunk, its prince with it.

"He is skilled with the sword, then?"

I ask the question but already know the answer.

When the queen, who was none too happy to learn of her husband's affair with one of her own ladies in waiting, insisted Aldwine's mother and the babe leave d'Almerita, the king reluctantly agreed. But he made provisions for the safety of the mother and son, hiring the most skilled swordsman of his day, a mercenary with a highly regarded reputation in both kingdoms to bring them to Murwood End.

Galfrid was pleased to learn of the marriage between his former lover and the mercenary, even more so because the man had returned the trunk of gold coin he'd been paid to escort her to Murwood End. Throughout the years, Galfrid sent men to Murwood End to check on the boy, now a man.

The boy was well cared for . . . until his father died in battle and his mother succumbed to the same sleeping illness that took my own parents. Though many healers claimed to know cures for the mysterious illness, every few years it seemed to sweep through Meria, tiring its victims, who then succumb to the longest sleep. Some are hardy on Sun's Day and dead by Wooden's Day. As it had been with both my mother and father.

"More skilled than any," Agnar says, snapping my attention back to him. "I'd give a goat's head to see you fight."

"No goat's head will be necessary. I look forward to honing my skills with any worthy opponent, yourself included."

Agnar grunts something that sounds like "thank ye," though I cannot be sure.

Remembering our first meeting, I ask a question that should probably be off-limits.

"Tell me of the blacksmith's daughter."

The good graces I'd gained with Agnar ebb away quickly. His look of displeasure is swift. But my need to know more about her overpowers my wish not to offend this man, even if he is of fine character and a decent swordsman.

"She's spoken for."

Mistrustful by nature, I don't believe him. But the tug in my chest at his words is unmistakable.

"Oh? She didn't mention it."

"You've spoken with her again?"

"Aye." I offer no more than that. "She is betrothed, then?" Another grunt. So I try a different question. "'Tis odd for me to see a Garra practice so openly. In Meria, they hide in the shadows."

Agnar shrugs. "Southerners have many strange customs."

"So there are none here who speak against it?"

"Her father, though he's too fond of her to put up much of a fuss. The Elderman, when he comes. None other."

"The Elderman?"

Agnar sheathes his sword and peers around the building, as if looking for someone. Perhaps he just wishes for an excuse to end our talk.

"Father Beald. His mission, to bring a church to Murwood, brings him to our shores a few times every year. They say he came this morning on The Talisman."

Something about the way he says it makes me think I should pay a visit to this Elderman. Clearly, he is a threat to Aedre. Which makes him a threat to me.

She needs no protection, but I will give it anyway.

"And her father?"

I should not have gone to him this morn, but I wanted to meet the man for myself.

"Fears for her." Another shrug. "Her grandmother no longer serves Murwood, but she has treated many here, parents and grandparents of the Voyagers. I did not know Aedre's mother, but they say she was quite a woman, like Lady Edrys. None would think to disparage her, or her granddaughter. But our ports bring in outsiders who know nothing of her history."

As if realizing he's said too much, Agnar abruptly stops talking. "Aedre is spoken for," he says again, more firmly this time. "Her father can handle a sword as well."

I'm undaunted by the unsubtle threat. If anything, I am more curious than before, both about this Elderman and Agnar's claim that she is taken.

Though if she is spoken for, it matters naught to me.

A woman such as Aedre, who clearly despises me, has no place in my world. My duty is to the king, the man who saved me and whose protection I've devoted my life to because of it.

CHAPTER ELEVEN
AEDRE

*L*ast eve, we agreed to meet at the same time, in the same place. I felt restless today, however, and I left before the shadows indicated it was time. No matter. This place, close to the village but distant enough to see few visitors, is one I've come to since childhood.

Amma and I sat on this very rock. This is where she told me of the natural powers of the stones that can be found along the shoreline. How healing could be conferred to the body by their power alone. And then, at night, looking up to the stars, she explained how their arrangement in the sky determined which plants to pick at various times.

With the arrival of a physician who came from Midenear, an island north of Murwood, Amma and I were free to practice the traditional healing arts of the Garra, focusing on ailments affecting the heart. From difficulty conceiving a child to stimulating lust for sexual intercourse.

I watch the water crash against the Cliffs of Murh to my left, remembering when Amma deemed me of age to treat such problems. Very much against my father's wishes, she'd long ago explained sexual intercourse, its importance unequivocal for the furthering of our people.

My smile deepens as I remember their argument, Father explaining he understood the merits of the Garra's duty, having married one. He just did not believe his daughter should be learning such things.

"You are quite beautiful when you smile."

Startled, I sit up straighter and offer Vanni a frown.

"How did you arrive here so quietly?"

This is the first time I've seen him without armor. Not even a padded gambeson. He wears just breeches and a loose cream shirt, wide open at the neck. Although his sword, ever present, is still at his side.

If I'm more beautiful with a smile, his has a similar effect. He looked less royal, less threatening. Dressed casually, hair damp from washing or a swim, Vanni d'Abella appears more like a Voyager than a Southerner today.

"I've many skills, my lady. Stealth is just one of them."

He sits in the same place as before, after unsheathing his sword and placing it next to him. The vulnerability he's showing me does not go unnoticed. He's far enough away that we are not touching, but close enough for me to smell his scent. A pleasant one, though pleasant is not the word I would use for him, precisely.

Striking.

Intent.

Very handsome.

Lord d'Abella must be quite popular with the ladies at court.

"You wished me to instruct you on our ways," I say. "But it seems my counsel is not necessary. Already I hear your name whispered throughout the village."

"Whispered by your intended?"

Since all spoke of Vanni's victories, including his match

against Agnar, who is considered our finest swordsman, save Kipp, I have no need to ask where he got that information.

"Agnar wishes it were so," I say, annoyed. "He should not have said that to you." I'd told myself he'd moved on, but clearly we were due another conversation.

"So 'tis not true?"

I do not mistake his tone this time. Nor the firm eye contact he's making, which I'm unwilling to break.

Oh, this man is dangerous to me.

I knew it from the very start, yet here I am anyway. A moth to a flame.

"Nay, not at all. Agnar is a friend, nothing more."

I could not presume to guess his thoughts on what passes between us then, an unspoken awareness that my body refuses to refute.

But his question prompts one of my own, for I've treated many whose only affliction is a willingness to warm marital beds other than their own.

"What of you? Are you not promised?"

His laugh is quick, harsh.

"Nay. Nor will I ever be."

I wet my lips, which are suddenly dry as stone.

"So says the man who has acquired the services of a Garra."

Vanni's eyes crinkle at the corners. "Marriage is very different than . . ." He stumbles.

"Sex. You may say the word. 'Tis not blasphemy to my ears."

His amusement only grows.

"Forgive me, Aedre. I'm unaccustomed to speaking with a woman so openly."

"A Garra," I correct him. "My mother and grandmother, and theirs before them, have taught me there is no shame in the very act which ensures our continued survival as a people."

He considers my words. "Then you know marriage is not necessary for sexual relations. But you also know that my . . . affliction was a pretense for these meetings."

I nod, for I know it well. "Why do you not plan to marry? Will it not be necessary to carry on your name?"

He shrugs, unconcerned. "My name will mean little if our kingdom does not remain secure. My duty is to the king."

A loud clap of water against the cliffs captures our attention. A storm is coming.

"So you will never marry?"

His answer is immediate. "I do not plan to do so."

Why does his answer annoy me so? I decide the wording is what grates on me, not the sentiment, so I say, "The heart does not plan. Love does not adhere to one's will."

Vanni looks to the sky and breathes in. The air is more pungent, the winds changing.

"When do you think the storm will arrive?" he asks.

So he will ignore my words about love, ones I should never have uttered. He is a noble. Of course he does not believe in love. Southerners marry for advantage, believing matters of the heart mean very little.

But our traditions are different.

"Soon," I say.

"I would ask questions of you today. Two, if I may. In exchange, I will grant you answers to two of your own."

His words startle me. Two questions of me. Aye, I would agree to that.

"Very well."

"You said you were raised here, in Murwood, with Aldwine. What do you know of him?"

I've thought much about this, and while I'd never give away Kipp's secrets, it's obvious Vanni already knows about his parentage. Kipp bears no love for the father who cast him aside.

Though King Galfrid has never sent his own Curia here before. That the second-highest-ranking man from court should come . . .

And yet, I cannot outright say what I know, if only because I promised Kipp I'd never speak of it. So I settle for a vague answer.

"I know everything there is to know. We are quite close."

His eyes widen. "Close?"

I realize he mistook my meaning. For some reason, I feel the need to correct him. "Our parents enjoyed a friendship that saw Kipp and I raised akin to brother and sister."

"You meet with me to protect him?" he correctly guesses, and I add *shrewd* to the ever-growing list of Vanni's traits.

He speaks into the silence that follows his question. "You know of his father?"

"I do."

"Not the mercenary."

"Nay, not the mercenary." I pause. "But the very man you serve."

His shoulders rise and fall, and for a horrifying moment, I wonder if I've misjudged the situation entirely. If he didn't know. If he was sent out here unwittingly, like the others, to check on Kipp. How could I blurt out one of my most precious secrets as if it were nothing?

"Aldwine has never told anyone before. Rumor of it would have spread far and wide."

I could weep with relief. "And he's told no one now, except my family. Kipp does not recognize the king as his father."

To clear up his confusion, I condemn myself even further. "As I said, his mother and my family were quite close. In town, none other than my grandmother, my father, and me know of Kipp's true origin."

He allowed me two questions, but I need only one.

"What do you want of him?"

Vanni considers what to tell me. So I share another secret.

"I have been taught not to trust those in power, and you, the king's Curia Commander, are such a man."

The slight lift of his lips on one side shows Vanni's amusement at my words. They are not meant to be amusing.

"And yet," I continue, "I told you a most treasured secret, one I have little right to tell."

"Because you realized I knew it already."

I shift on the hard rock, bothered less by the discomfort— I've sat on this very stone for hours and hours—than by Vanni's ever-present gaze. Desire, I know, is both natural and necessary. Even so, I've never felt more than a twinge of it before.

Yet now, without herbs or stones or words of encouragement or any of the other enticements we use, my body screams for his touch. The longer he looks at me so, the more I wish for it.

"Perhaps."

"Very well." He looks out at the increasingly turbulent sea. "You'll learn soon enough of the events unfolding in the south. Your honesty for my own."

He sits up and leans slightly toward me. We aren't touching, but it wouldn't take much to change that—he need only move slightly forward.

"You know of the fighting along the borders?"

I nod. "Of course."

Though the Terese River has separated Edingham from Meria since the Treaty of Loigh, formed nearly thirty years after the two kingdoms split, it does little to quell the unrest that has plagued the borders.

"And of the attack on Saitford?"

News of the border town's trouble has reached us. Although violence along the Meria-Edingham border is not a new occurrence. "Aye."

Murwood might lie on the north side of the Loigh Mountains, apart from either kingdom, but ships bring not only cargo but news. We know much of what happens in both Meria and Edingham.

"They say a Highlander set fire to it," I say, "killing a mother and her children in the blaze."

Vanni is no longer smiling. "More than one mother and her child. The fire, set in the dead of night, claimed nearly half of those who lived in Saitford."

I shudder, thankful we see little fighting along our shores.

"King Galfrid mounted a retaliatory attack on Edingham."

"An occurrence as old as the split between the kingdoms."

He frowns. "This would have seen more than two hundred of his best soldiers near Galmouth Bay."

Despite myself, I'm drawn in. I've not heard of such a sizable attack.

"*Would* have seen?"

Because I am trained to see emotions more than most, I can already tell Vanni is preparing to share something extremely painful to him.

"A new ship, its captain one of the most renowned in Meria, was commissioned. But it sank not long after leaving the shore."

A fluttering in my belly intensifies.

"The king's son was among those who perished. The Prince of Meria is dead."

My hand rushes to cover my mouth. A quick calculation tells me precisely why Vanni is here. I know of the king's nephew, whose reputation is as bleak as his father's. Even those who dislike King Galfrid acknowledge he's a far better man than his brother. Whereas words like "fair" and "honorable" are used to describe the king, his nephew is known for being treacherous and cruel. Capricious. It's little wonder the king is so anxious to avoid naming him successor. Which brings me to my next question.

"Is the king prepared to recognize Kipp as his successor?"

My guess is met with a nod. "Aye."

"He will not do it." Blurted before I can think better of it, my words don't seem to surprise Vanni at all.

"I'm told he cares little for his father."

"For the man who abandoned him and his mother?" I ask. "Nay, he does not."

"Galfrid loved Aldwine's mother, and the queen knew it well. She would never have allowed her to remain in d'Almerita. He sent her away with coin and protection. And has not failed in all these years to ensure his well-being."

"Lord Hinton will be your next king," I say. It is not a question. Kipp has heard all of those arguments before. None will sway his thinking.

"He cannot be."

I agree, such a state is not desirable for Meria. Or, truly, for any of us. But Kipp is as stubborn as the king is purported to be. He will never agree to meet with the man, let alone take his crown.

"You've been sent on a fool's errand."

"Perhaps."

We fall silent. As Vanni admires the looming Cliffs of Murh, I admire his profile, his strong jaw, now clenched in frustration.

"You visited my father this morn. Why?"

He turns back to me. "Your second question?"

"Perhaps."

"To appease my curiosity."

"About me?"

"Aye."

He is a nobleman. A king's man. A Southerner. Even so, I feel myself being drawn to him. His openness today only makes him more appealing.

"I've not met a woman like you before, Aedre."

His words do little to calm my rapidly beating heart.

"A Garra?"

"Nay. A woman. Garra or no."

How easy it would be to let myself be charmed by him. Fooled into trusting where I shouldn't. I look to the dark, roiling sky.

"We should go."

My words come too late. Two small drops appear on the rock in front of us. We stand as more appear. By the time we climb over the rocks, drops have begun to fall in earnest.

"Take off your boots," I say, unlacing my own as quickly as I can. I don't wait to see if Vanni listens to me. I hike up my skirts with one hand and cling to my boots with the other as I run across the sand rather than toward the village.

For this will be no light rain, and the village is much too far for us to reach without getting drenched. Indeed, we should have left the shore much earlier.

When I reach the cave's entrance, I peer inside, knowing it will be empty but needing to reassure myself of it. Entering, then turning back, I see a very virile Vanni standing under the rocky archway, framed by the angry sea beyond him.

CHAPTER TWELVE

VANNI

*T*his does not bode well.

My thoughts are increasingly absorbed by the woman standing before me, boots in one hand, skirts in another. If our rock perch felt intimate, safe from prying eyes, this seaside cave is even more so.

Which reminds me . . .

"You take too many chances with a stranger," I warn her. "Leaving the village. Coming to this place." I place my own boots on a large rock, my sword following it there.

A crack of thunder follows my words, bringing a heavy rain with it.

"Would you prefer for us to be stuck in that?" Aedre adds her own boots to my collection.

Rolling my breeches up, I don't relent. "For a woman who trusts Southerners so little, you have put yourself in a dangerous position. Being alone with me in here."

Neither of us move.

"I could rape you."

"But you will not."

"Another man might."

"I've seen twenty-five summers without being touched by a man. Surely I can continue to defend myself without your guidance."

"Never been touched by a man?" I repeat, the words more of a challenge than any I've faced with my sword.

"In the way you speak of."

Ah. Which means . . .

"But you have been kissed?"

Not my question to ask, but I do so anyway.

"'Tis none of your concern."

Aedre's annoyance is obvious. Mayhap she resents my meddling, my unwanted warnings. But I suspect there's more to it.

Another loud crack fills the cave. Although not deep, it's wide, and the stone overhead high enough to easily accommodate us. Only a few steps would bring me to her.

"I don't wish to insult you."

"Would you tell one of your men not to find himself alone with another even for the sake of staying dry?"

I am about to remind her my men are, in fact, men, when I remember her trick with the knife.

"You surprised me once, but it would not happen again."

Aedre rolls her eyes, obviously annoyed by the discussion.

"You will not rape me, so can we stop speaking of it?"

"And you know this for a fact?"

"Aye."

"How do you know it?" She is right, of course, but I still wish for her to understand the danger.

"Though a Southerner and a noble, you are also an honorable man."

She says it with such disgust, as if she wished it were not so, and I laugh.

"You believe so?"

"Aye."

Aedre doesn't explain the basis for her judgment, but since her words are indeed accurate, I've no argument to give.

Instead, sitting beside my belongings, I say, "Tell me of the Elderman."

Aedre moves toward me and hikes up her skirts as she takes a seat, giving me a brief glimpse of her bare legs before I look away. When I imagined this journey, not once did I consider the possibility of finding myself trapped in a seaside cave during a raging storm with a beautiful Garra.

"Father Beald is a hateful man who wishes to establish a church here in Murwood."

"He does not know your history well, then."

When the kingdoms split, a group of men and women who disagreed with some of the views of King Onry of Meria's second son came here. Determined not to allow the Prima and his army of religious men to control them as King Onry had, they took to the sea for trade. Only years later, when both kingdoms accepted they would not be able to claim Murwood End as their own after many failed attempts, did they open once again to trade with those who inhabit their own island.

Voyagers were born. Their ties to Meria, Edingham, and certainly to the church, were severed.

"He is a fool. But a dangerous one."

"How is that?"

It strikes me this is the first time I've seen a look of hatred on Aedre's face. She's never looked at me this way, not even when we first met.

"He has the ear of the Prima."

Father Silvester.

From humble beginnings in Galona, he rose through the ranks of the church like an arrow, once even managing to convince the king to award him the port town of Avalon, now the seat of the church in Meria. The man's ambition is endless. Galfrid dislikes him but is forced to tolerate him. The church's involvement in both kingdoms has caused more tension than not throughout the years.

"I will speak with him."

Aedre startles. "Why?"

For a simple reason. "Because he scares you."

She opens her mouth to argue but then shuts it again. The truth of my words is evident to us both. I've no need to ask the reason. Though it's been some time since the Garra were openly persecuted, their history of harassment at the hands of the church is long and storied.

"I commit no crime here."

"Nor would you be considered a criminal if you were in Meria. But that does not stop him from harassing you."

She does not deny my words, which means I am due a stern discussion with this Elderman. While Galfrid is still king, Silvester's men are not to torment our people. Even the Voyagers of Murwood, who do not recognize any authority beyond their own.

"You cannot do such a thing."

"I can, and I will."

As we speak, the rain begins to slow. The beauty of the moment strikes me. Aedre is beside me, framed by the opening of the cave: a wall of water, only sand and sea beyond it.

When I look at Aedre, she is gifting me with a rare smile.

"You think highly of your skills."

"Just my connection to men your Elderman would rather not anger." I find it necessary to add, "I am not the enemy, Aedre. I've no wish to harm you or your grandmother.

You'll find most Southerners more tolerant than you believe."

"And some who are not."

I cannot refute her words.

"You've no dishonorable men or women here in Murwood?"

Her chin rises. "Aye. But even the most dishonorable among them understand the danger of being beholden to the whims of kings or Eldermen."

The rain stops as quickly as it started, but neither of us move. Looking at her here, in the murky light of the cave, the distance between us so small, I wonder again what it would be like to kiss her. She's been touched by a man before, but how?

Does it matter?

I will leave when Aldwine returns, never to see her again. Surprisingly, the thought of leaving her untouched, of leaving her forever, is unsettling.

"That very look has gotten young women with babes in their belly."

Caught by surprise again, I laugh. "Has it now? A fine Garra you are indeed, if you think 'tis done that way."

I stand, and she does so with me.

"I know how 'tis done," she says, smiling.

Two smiles in one afternoon. It is a miracle indeed.

"I'll not deny my desire for you, Aedre. 'Tis plain to see, as you've pointed out."

As is hers for me. I suspected before, but now I'm sure.

"And yet, you restrain yourself. 'Tis why I knew I would be safe with you in here. You've looked at me thus since the first time we met. But we've been alone before, and you've never once tried anything."

Her forthrightness only makes her more desirable.

I take out a coin purse and move toward her. "Will you

meet me on the morrow? I've gotten to know much of Murwood from our meetings."

I take her hand. Aedre does not pull it away.

Unprepared for the spark such innocent contact ignites, I place the small bag in her palm and step back as if scorched.

"You do not need me," she says softly.

She's wrong. So very wrong.

I've lived only to serve Galfrid these many years. But being with Aedre reminds me of what I've given up . . . a life of my own.

"Help me gain an audience with him."

Aedre moves past me to take hold of her boots. My eyes linger on her backside, but I glance away quickly as she turns.

"He will be wroth with me for it."

"I know you care little for Meria, but you are a healer, Aedre. Your nature is to help people. If Lord Hinton becomes king, all will suffer."

I remember one fact about the sinking which we did not discuss earlier.

"He was on the ship that day. The king's nephew. He was to sail with it, but after too much revelry the eve before, the simple act of standing on deck was too much for him. Before it went to sea, Hinton disembarked. The church, seeing his survival as a sign he should be named as successor, immediately offered him their support. I left only days after the king's son perished, but already word of Hinton as the church's chosen one had spread."

"Despite the man's nature?"

If she is incredulous, we were as much so.

"You know their teachings as well as I. They claim God's will can only be interpreted through signs they alone can read. They consider this the ultimate sign of his will: sparing a man who should have perished."

She watches me for any glimmer of deceit. But there is none.

"I ask just for an audience."

"And if he refuses to leave with you?"

"Then we go without him. We've no edict to force him, nor would our interests be served in doing so. No man can be made to accept the crown."

"How can you know what kind of king he would be?"

The question is an easy one to answer. "Galfrid has kept watch over him for many years. Would you deny he'd make a good king to Meria?"

Wetting her lips, though an innocent gesture, makes me forget for a moment about my mission, my attention snared by the possibility that Aedre may allow me to kiss her before I leave Murwood.

Just once.

It is a weakness I never knew existed in me. Every one of my previous dalliances has been with widows or women not tied to the precarious strings of nobility. Never have I compromised a woman before, or even considered doing so. Perhaps this weakness was simply waiting for Aedre to release it.

"Nay, I cannot deny it. Very well."

My jaw drops. I'd not expected her to agree so easily.

"But there is no longer any need for us to meet. You need nothing else from me, except this one boon. Which I grant as a grateful gesture for your offer to speak to the Elderman."

I'm grateful for her agreement, less so for her decision to no longer meet with me.

We stare at each other for a moment, so close it would be an easy thing to pull her to me, but I don't. The moment passes, and Aedre flees from the cave as quickly as she did from the rock by the shore.

I decide her habit of fleeing is not my favorite thing about her.

You do not need me.

True or not, it matters little. Aedre has spoken, and I've little else to do but heed her words. Though I have gained something extremely valuable this day, an audience with the future king of Meria.

CHAPTER THIRTEEN

AEDRE

"*D*o you suppose it will work?"

I hand the mixture to the midwife and bid her to drink it.

"Better than placing fish inside you. Where did you learn such nonsense?"

My friend Aloisa has a sheepish look. She's only been the town midwife for less than a year. Before her mother's death, she didn't show much interest in the calling, but she's since become a fine midwife. Except for her belief in tall tales.

"You know more about women's bodies than most. Can you not see 'tis a silly notion?"

Aloisa drank the mixture I gave her and placed the empty cup on the table next to her. She and her husband share a modest two-story, timber-framed cottage right in the very center of the village, but a short walk for me. And so we visit each other often.

But this is no casual meeting.

When Aloisa first told me she was having difficulty becoming pregnant, I was more surprised than I should have been. If I can practice as a Garra, never having been in love myself, then surely a midwife could have difficulty with the very thing she practices every day.

"'Tis not magic, Aloisa, as well you know. The mixture will simply relax you, for I'm sure your worry is not easing matters."

Amma believes pleasure during sexual relations is not a sin. And that it can even be beneficial to conception. Aloisa is likely too overwhelmed by her concerns to find any joy in the act, and I'm hopeful the mixture I've given her will indeed help.

"A fish . . . ," I begin.

The very idea.

"Aedre." Aloisa's husband opens the door and steps inside. A fisherman, he most often does not return home until much later in the evening. But the storm that arrived yesterday has lingered. It is raining even now, so I put up my hood before venturing outside.

"Are you well?" I ask.

"Well indeed." He stops me as I make to leave. "You may wish to wait, the rain will be coming down harder soon."

Though I adore them both, I do not wish to be trapped here all eve, nor does Aloisa wish it, I suspect, from the way she is looking at her husband.

Offering a silent blessing, I make toward the door.

"Then I shall hurry. Good eve to you both."

Closing the door behind me, I walk quickly.

But not quickly enough. Just as I pass Sailor's Inn, the rain falls as heavily as if someone were standing above me pouring brimming buckets over my head.

Ducking inside the tavern portion of the inn, I wonder if I made the best choice. Will it indeed rain all eve? If so, I shall simply walk home after a quick meal, resigned to remain wet.

I turn, my eyes adjusting to the dim light of candles and few lanterns, the shutters closed to ward off the rain. Then I make my way to the back of the great room and sit on a stool at the long board. I'm not far from the table where I sat with Vanni.

"Beef stew for ya, Aedre girl?"

The innkeeper himself slides a mug of ale toward me without asking. Father and I have come here many times throughout the years, the owner Neill, having been a friend of his since childhood.

"Aye, if it pleases you."

"Pleases me plenty." The old man shuffles off, leaving me to my thoughts, but is back again before long.

"Our finest bowl of stew, my lady."

"Many thanks." I toss two coins onto the board. "'Tis less crowded than I'd have thought, with the rain."

Instead of answering, Neill looks behind me. So I turn, my heart thumping with the hope that Vanni might be behind me. But I groan as soon as I see the man making his way toward me.

"Father Beald."

"A woman alone in an establishment such as this would be heartily frowned upon in many places," he comments, giving me a look full of judgment.

I glance around for Neill, but I'm not the only one who dislikes the Elderman. He's nowhere to be seen. I've been left to ward off the Elderman myself.

"Much like a man of God who preaches love and spews hate."

I've attempted in the past to garner the man's favor despite his obvious dislike for me, but no honeyed words can overcome blind hatred. I had long ago stopped trying.

His smirk makes my blood run cold.

"You've left Murwood End to learn the truth of your words?"

I've not. And he knows it well.

Leaning toward me, he whispers for my ears alone. "I've visited your grandmother. The great Lady Edrys did not appear very well. Such a shame. So few Garra remain. I shouldn't be surprised if there's one less one day soon."

Tensing, I do not even attempt to hide the anger that courses through me.

"You are an evil man."

He does not seem the least bit bothered by my words.

"The only evil here, Lady Aedre, is a brazen woman who preaches pleasure. Who caters to the devil's whims, flaunting herself as if proud. And proud of what? You are less than nothing."

I want to flee. To rid myself of his presence. But I can't allow him that victory. So I turn back to my ale as if his words do not make me want to toss the contents of my mug in his face.

After a moment, no longer able to feel his cloying presence next to me, I glance over my shoulder, wholly unprepared to see Vanni standing between us.

He says something to the Elderman, who, with one final glare back at me, turns to leave. It comes as little surprise when Vanni follows him out.

Attempting to steady my hands, which are still shaking, I take a drink. And another. Only when a second ale is placed in front of me, Neill apologizing for leaving when he sees my face, does Vanni return. He does not say a word but rather nods to the table where we sat several days earlier, one affording more privacy.

"That will be the last time Father Beald speaks to you again."

I'm not prepared for the controlled anger that simmers

beneath the surface of his words. But then, neither am I prepared for another conversation with the man I've thought about nearly every moment since leaving that cave.

Vanni sits and leans forward across the table.

"Tell me what he said to you."

CHAPTER FOURTEEN
VANNI

*T*his was the closest I've come to injuring a man of God.

I fought a Shadow Warrior once, a guest of Castle d'Almerita. Though Father Aiken arrived with the Prima, I immediately sensed something different about him. While many of the Eldermen and their warriors shared their leader's extreme views, this one held his tongue during his time as the king's guest.

Father Aiken and I challenged each other each day of his visit. He defeated me the first day. And I him, on the second.

As I got to know the man, I found there was little to dislike. Our beliefs were different, but he was a good, honorable man, and one of the best warriors I'd ever had the pleasure of fighting.

So I know there are good men and bad in the church. But I am equally certain Father Beald belongs to the latter group. He is no warrior, however, so I could not challenge him as I did Father Aiken. I had to use words, and the ones I chose were sharper than any blade. The Elderman, as I said to Aedre, promised never again to return to Murwood End.

"How did you know he was bothering me?"

I take a deep, steadying breath. So much for my reputation for even temperament. Still angry, I remind myself it is over. He won't bother her again.

"I saw you as soon as I came in."

I don't tell her that it was as if I felt her presence. Nonsense, of course, but I was not surprised to see her here.

"Your expression."

Aedre says nothing but pulls her ale closer.

"What did he say to you?"

I drink, waiting for her answer. It takes a moment for her to speak.

"'I've visited your grandmother,'" she finally says, her voice cracking. "'The great Lady Edrys did not appear very well. Such a shame. So few Garra remain. I shouldn't be surprised if there's one less one day soon.'"

I almost regret making her repeat it.

"Aedre . . ."

Wanting to comfort her, knowing I cannot, I choose instead to explain my own exchange with Father Beald. I glance around before speaking, but no one is paying us any mind. Our table is at a distance from the others, as intimate a setting as possible in the midst of a small hall.

"King Galfrid has little patience for Father Silvester." I lower my voice to a whisper. "Their relationship has been strained for years, and it will only worsen if the church attempts to interfere in the naming of a successor."

"Their recommendation of Lord Hinton, you mean."

"Aye. But even so, Silvester needs the king's support, and for the time being that king is still Galfrid. He's threatened to take away Avalon before. Nearly did so last winter. I simply reminded Beald of my position at court and of Galfrid and Silvester's tenuous relationship."

Her eyes widen.

"The king would excommunicate the Prima from Meria?"

I pause, looking at her stew. After a long day of training, more and more locals challenging me in wake of my defeat of Agnar, the smell prompts me to ask for a bowl as well as a serving maid walks by.

"Eat," I say when she pauses.

Aedre picks up the pewter spoon, and I try not to watch her lips too closely as they open. Imagine, to be jealous of a beef stew. Shifting in my seat, I force my eyes upward.

Since she sees me clearly, I don't hide the direction of my thoughts.

"What were we discussing?" I say.

Amused, she takes another bite of stew.

"Ah, yes." I lower my voice, even though we sit at a distance from any others. The shutters are closed, but the sound of heavy rain still penetrates. A low murmur of conversation and the fire in the hearth make this particular inn, and this moment, more peaceful a setting than I'd imagined I would find in Murwood End.

As a boy, this place seemed ominous, almost scary to me. Now, it holds a tantalizing feeling of possibility. The people here are notoriously fierce, independent, and wary of strangers, this particular woman more so than most. I'd expected to be here for a very short time, wishing every moment to leave.

Now, I'd prefer to be here than any other place on the Isle.

"We were discussing nothing more than the excommunication of the Prima from Meria," I continue, shaking myself from my thoughts.

"Just so."

My own stew arrives, and I thank the serving girl for it.

"To answer your question, aye, he would. I simply reminded Beald of the situation, hinted that he would learn of further discord in coming days, and asked if he really wished to contribute to faltering relations."

Finally, she pushes her bowl away. "You threatened him."

"Aye."

"Because of me."

I finish chewing. A fine stew, though different than what I'm accustomed to.

"Aye, because of you. Because I dislike the man. And because Galfrid would be as intolerant of him as I am."

She seems surprised to hear it. Aedre thinks little of the king, a fact which I hope to alter.

"You believe so?"

"I know it. You accused me of antiquated notions, and perhaps the role of women here is different than in the south. But neither Galfrid nor I tolerate injustice. He is an honorable man, Aedre. Why do you think so little of him?"

I eat, content to listen to her explanation.

"He allowed his wife to cast out his son to the farthest reaches of the kingdom. A father who abandons his child can have no redemption in my eyes."

Reminded of her close friendship to Aldwine, I choose my words carefully.

"For his own protection. The queen is not known for her tolerance. And Aldwine's mother *chose* to flee to Murwood End. The king did not require it."

My men come inside, soaking wet. Seeing us, they speak among themselves and disappear up the stairs, presumably to their rooms. I do not need to guess what they think of my friendship, as it were, with Aedre.

They've not ceased their jests about the matter since we arrived.

"The king married her, did he not?" she says loftily.

"The marriage was arranged."

"He made the choice."

"Nay, he had none. Choice is a privilege, Aedre, reserved for some." She clearly disagrees with me. "There is another side to him as well. A generous one. He brought me up in Castle d'Almerita after both of my parents died."

I told her not for sympathy but to prove my point, and yet Aedre's eyes fill with tears. "How did they die?"

"The sleeping illness. My father served the king."

I can see she understands why I'll not be swayed by her words against him. Like any man, Galfrid has made mistakes. But he is a good man, one who cares deeply for others, much like Aedre.

She would not risk herself to practice as a Garra otherwise.

"My mother died in childbirth."

I stop eating, but Aedre forges ahead.

"My father is overprotective because of it. But I'm grateful for his love. And for my grandmother."

Not knowing what to say, I finish the stew in silence. Not an awkward silence, but a companionable one, shared by two people who know the pain of not having a complete family.

The crack of thunder reminds me of being with her in that cave. The desire to reach out and touch her is nearly overwhelming.

When the serving maid takes away my bowl and slams down a tankard of ale, apologizing for it slipping from her hand, Aedre and I exchange a glance.

"'Tis still raining," I comment.

"Aye."

"Can you stay or will your father worry?"

I refill my mug, waiting for her to answer.

"He will know I've taken shelter. I can stay."

I still don't move.

"Do you want to stay? The other day you said you no longer wished to see me."

I've thought of nothing else these past few days—the glances Aedre stole when she didn't think I was looking, the feeling of connection we had, and the way she left me in that cave without a backward glance.

A woman like no other.

"I said 'twas not necessary for you to retain my services." Aedre nods to the mug. "Nothing more."

I fill her mug, hope swelling inside me.

Perhaps I should feel guilty for enjoying myself so thoroughly with Meria on the verge of collapse, but I push such ominous thoughts aside.

I may not have time for a woman such as Aedre back at d'Almerita, but for the few days I remain in Murwood End? I savor the thought of more pleasant conversations with this extraordinary woman.

Even if I'd prefer much, much more.

CHAPTER FIFTEEN
AEDRE

*I*t's dark now, and the rain has stopped. Father no doubt will be looking for me. Though I don't wish to leave, it is time.

"I will walk you home."

We stand in front of the Sailor's Inn, the docks quiet after the storm. I hold onto my skirts in order not to muddy the hem, an effort sure to end in failure.

"I've made the journey alone many, many times. 'Tis safe enough for me here."

None in the village would harm me.

"It may be safe, but still, I would walk you home."

Father will certainly learn of the time we spent this eve, for enough people saw Vanni and I together that someone is sure to tell him of it. Perhaps he might worry less knowing the commander is an honorable man.

I need no protection, but Father does not always agree.

So I simply nod and lead the way toward the vast darkness that is the Merian Sea. We walk in silence along the water, and I think on what I've learned about Vanni this day.

His parents' death and his upbringing at Castle d'Almerita. Three things have become clear this day.

For one, he loves the king as he would a father. The reasons are plain enough, and I'm anxious to speak to Amma about his revelations. She is as mistrustful of King Galfrid as anyone, yet the man Vanni describes is not the monster Kipp believes his father to be.

I've also learned my mistrust of all nobles may have been misplaced. I know Vanni will not share my secrets, just as I would never share his.

Last, I now know what desire feels like, not only how it makes people behave. The stirrings I've experienced in the past are like ripples in the sea compared to the thunderous waves that now crash within me.

I think of him when I wake and when I lay my head down to sleep. I imagine my hand in his, the dark waves of his hair, or his thick arms encircling me. It's why I fled from that cave, scared to remain in such close proximity to him. I know how quickly desire can spiral out of control. Many a maid, a babe in her belly, only thought to steal a simple kiss.

"When do you think Aldwine will return?"

The moon shines brightly before us, illuminating our path.

"Soon," I say, stealing a glance at Vanni. "Though I meant what I said. He will not return to the south with you."

I say it not to antagonize him, but because it is almost certainly the truth.

"If he does not, I fear for the kingdom."

"Is Lord Hinton as horrible as the rumors suggest?"

I've heard enough over the years from traders to know he would not be an ideal leader.

"When his father, the king's brother, died, Hinton refused to lay him to rest. Said he'd done him no favors and could rot in hell despite the fact that father and son are very much alike. The man is truly despicable. And yet, the church intends to back him anyway. It's maddening."

The sound of water lapping against the docks lulls us back into our companionable silence. Turning away from the water, we walk toward the outer buildings of our small village. When we hired a maidservant a few years ago, my father said he could rest easy, having achieved far more than he'd ever thought possible.

"Is that it there?" He points into the distance.

"Aye." I stop, contemplating.

"Father would be pleased you've accompanied me. However . . ."

We're just behind the mill, hidden well enough now, but we will be easily seen once we enter the open field. If we are to part ways, now would be the time.

And yet, I'm reluctant for Vanni to leave.

"I will watch you from here," he says courteously.

"You are not what I expected." The words leave my lips before I can think better of it.

"Our ways are different, Lady Aedre, but we can teach each other."

That very statement proves my point. It is exactly the last thing I'd have presumed to hear from a man raised at court to serve a king.

"I've met few nobles, and even fewer of your ilk," I admit.

Thankfully, Vanni does not seem inclined to leave just yet.

"We are not all bad, Aedre." He says it softly, without censure.

My chest constricts when he takes a step toward me, tall enough that I'm forced to look up. His eyes seem to be pleading for something.

For me to believe his words, that he is not the man I thought him to be?

His lips part, and I realize his plea is of a different kind.

Although I've thought of this moment many times over the last few days, of what it might feel like to kiss him, I know it would be a fleeting pleasure. As he has said, he will be leaving, with or without Kipp. And yet, I want to do it anyway. I gulp the air, thick still with the remnants of the storm.

"I would kiss you, Aedre."

I want that too. But I can't find the words. Fine Garra I've proven to be. My vocation is to help others with love, only the desire I feel for this man has filled me with longing and fear.

Longing for a man who would do as right by me as he would the king he serves.

Fear at the knowledge that I would enjoy the kiss. That I would want more.

Where would such a foolhardy act leave me? With an eternal ache in my heart for what could have been had the king's commander been any other man?

"You will leave any day," I accuse.

"Aye."

"How many women have you kissed in moments such as this?"

I imagine a trail of women, from Murwood down to the capital, wishing for just one more glance, one more touch, from Lord Vanni d'Abella.

"Not as many as you believe it to be."

My questions seem to be enough of an answer for him. Vanni steps back, and the heat between us dissipates into a cold chill.

His chin rises. "Apologies, my lady."

But he doesn't move to leave—he's waiting for me to walk away.

Should I tell him that my hesitation is because I fear a

fleeting moment of pleasure will curse me with visions of him after he leaves? Even now, without such intimacies, I fear his face will be one I see for some time.

What could he say to that?

Nothing that would ease the sting of losing him.

And so, for the second time, I walk away. This time with a heavier heart than before. This afternoon was truly pleasurable.

"Good eve," I mutter, grasping my skirts even more tightly as I hurry toward home. I don't look back until I reach the gate which fences in our manor, the only home I remember. Once, we lived at the back of the forge. But as the years went on, my father and grandmother earned enough coin to build a small manor that better accommodates us all, and we moved here.

Turning, I strain to see him, but the fickle moon doesn't cast enough light. Though I don't see him, I do not need to. I'm as certain Vanni still waits there as I am my father and Amma will have many questions.

Well, I have questions for them as well. Though my father and grandmother disagree about my future, they've always held a united front in telling me powerful people have questionable motives.

Either Vanni is the rare exception or their warnings have been overzealous, making me wonder if any of my other long-held beliefs are mistaken.

CHAPTER SIXTEEN
VANNI

I hear her laughter before I see her. Not the tinkling laughter of one of the women at court, but a deep sound. A sound one could cherish, if given the chance.

I nearly reconsider my visit when a voice calls my name.

Sitting beside the forge, looking out toward the sea, a woman who must be her grandmother crooks a finger for me to come close.

Smoke billows from the building as I move toward her.

Lady Edrys has the kind of eyes that see through a person. She says nothing as I stand before her, waiting for her assessment.

"You are the commander."

Her voice is stronger than her body. Hunched slightly, her hands knotted on her lap, the Garra reminds me of the steward's wife at Castle d'Almerita, wise in a way that none who've lived a shorter time can match.

"Aye, my lady. Lord Vanni d'Abella, if it pleases you."

Bowing, I stand as she reaches out her hand.

I take it, not knowing what to expect. She turns my palm

up and holds it for some time. When she finally releases it, I feel as if she knows more of me than I do of her.

"You worry for Aedre," I guess, knowing she's told her grandmother a little about the time we've spent together.

"Always."

I try to reassure her. "I'd not dishonor your granddaughter, despite what you think of me."

She seems surprised by that.

"And what do I think of you, Lord d'Abella?"

My answer is swift. "That I disagree with your practice. I don't, though, and I would never seek to harm you or Aedre."

"Hmmm." She does not deny it.

"I've a purpose here, and 'tis not to persecute anyone."

Another "hmm" follows.

"Forgive me for being forward, but Aedre seemed to believe I'd wish her harm when we first met." Realizing I used her given name, I attempt to amend my words. "Lady Aedre. I mean no disrespect."

"I thought I heard your voice."

I turn . . . and immediately wish I hadn't. Seeing Aedre this way, her blacksmith's apron covering her, no gown today but a pair of men's breeches and shirt beneath it . . .

Her hair is piled atop her head. Hammer in hand.

God, what a woman.

"Good day, my lady. I'm here to check on the progress of my sword."

And to see you, for it seems I can't stay away, even when you wish it so.

The sound of iron banging against iron and the smell of smoke reminds me of the forge at the castle. The people of Murwood End may not bow to either king nor queen, but they've many of the same customs as we do. This forge could easily belong in the south.

"'Tis nearly finished. Come, see."

I nod to Lady Edrys, still uncertain of her thoughts about me.

"Does she always speak so little?" I whisper as we head into the forge.

"To strangers, aye."

Of course I am a stranger, and in most villages, outsiders are met with mistrust and unease. But I don't want to be a stranger to Aedre, or to those she holds dear.

"Ahh, Lord d'Abella."

Aedre gives the hammer to a young man, presumably the smith's apprentice, as her father wipes his hands on the front of his apron.

"I've finished your sword." He walks around us and, picking up my new weapon, hands it to me.

The pattern-welded core with welded-on cutting edges, typical of a Voyager sword, is the reason I asked for it to be made. Well, one of them.

"A fine sword indeed." I turn it over in my hand. "Your craftsmanship would be most desired in the capital. The master smith there is old, his hands feeble. His apprentice is young and not so skilled."

Aedre and her father exchange a glance that I don't quite understand.

Instead of guessing at its meaning, I set the sword aside and pull out the coin purse I'd prepared. Handing it to Master Dal, I'm surprised when he pushes it back toward me.

"Nay, I will not take your coin."

I look at Aedre, but she seems as surprised as I am.

"I do not understand," I say, attempting to give it to him again.

A shadow crosses the smith's face. Anger, barely concealed.

"Aedre told me about your conversation with Father Beald."

"I didn't take kindly to his threats. Nor would King Galfrid."

I want this man to trust me. Mayhap even like me. So I nod to the apprentice, and Aedre's father sends him off on an errand. Once the three of us are alone, I tell him what I confessed to Aedre, from the tragedy of the ship sinking to the threat posed by the king's nephew. And of course, to the role Kipp plays in all of it.

"He will not go with you."

Aedre gives me a *Did I not say so already?* look.

"If he does not, Galfrid will be forced to name another as heir. But I fear even the best of men will not be accepted before his own nephew."

"Especially since the church is backing him," Aedre adds.

"Aye."

I can tell from his expression Aedre had not yet relayed this information to her father.

"You came a long way, my lord, for little gain."

His words echo his daughter's, but my response is the same.

"He must." I try one final time to hand Master Dal the coin, but he pushes it back.

"You've given my family a great boon, if indeed the Elderman will stay away. Keep your coin."

I pick the sword back up, thanking him again for such fine craftsmanship.

"I wish you luck on your quest. Aedre can no doubt arrange a meeting, but do not expect Kipp to answer with anything but contempt."

She already has agreed to do so, and I'm learning as much.

With nothing more to keep me here, I thank the smith once again and turn to leave. Closing my eyes as I step outside, I attempt to calm the slamming of my heart in my chest.

"Vanni?"

She stops me just as I'm about to bid farewell to Lady Edrys.

When I spin around, she freezes. If my expression is too harsh, it's only because I'm struggling to control my reaction to her.

"Meet me at the rock?" she whispers.

No five words have ever sounded sweeter.

CHAPTER SEVENTEEN
AEDRE

I watch him for a moment as I approach. Vanni, sitting atop my rock, *our* rock, framed by the sea and the cliffs beyond. He looks peaceful, almost. And yet his skills with a sword are already infamous in Murwood End.

His men are skilled too, but Vanni did not become the king's commander simply because the king is fond of him. He obviously earned that right, and some are openly wondering if he could best Kipp.

No one could conceive of such a thing before Vanni arrived.

Kipp's father was so skilled with a sword he could have become a court advisor in Meria or Edingham. Instead, he chose the life of a mercenary . . . and did well enough he built Nord Manor.

I look toward it now, far off to the right, on a tidal island only accessible by foot at low tide. Watching its construction gave the people of Murwood End years of entertainment. The manor, and the man who owns it, represent the best of us.

Independent. Ruled by no one. Sometimes inaccessible but still bold and beautiful.

I look back to Vanni, who sees me and likely wonders why I don't join him. Or why I brought him here in the first place.

What should I say to him?

Despite the invitation I was so quick to give, I still don't know.

Amma and I talked well into the night, and her admission that Vanni may not be dangerous was tempered by a warning.

He may not wish you harm, my child. But pain takes many forms.

As a Garra, I know the truth of her words well. Even still, I walk toward him, compelled by a force stronger than my conflicted thoughts. Scrambling over small rocks to get to the large one, I greet Vanni as he stands.

My "good day" turns to something less intelligible as I stumble—and he easily catches me. I take his hand instinctively, his strong fingers wrapping around mine.

I've regained my balance, but he still doesn't let me go.

Unlike the last time we were here, today the sea is calm, a steady clapping of water on the rocks. There's something seductive about it. Coupled with Vanni's gaze and the heat of his hand, it urges me to get closer to him . . .

Without thinking of the consequences, I close the distance between us, looking up into his eyes. But unlike the evening before, I am no longer scared. Aye, he will leave in a few days. But if I must think of the king's commander when I sit upon this rock, then I will do so without regret.

"You ran from me," he says, still holding my hand. "Twice."

If there was anything I've ever wanted more than Vanni d'Abella to kiss me, I cannot remember it at this moment.

"I know better than others not to trifle with matters of the heart."

He takes my other hand, and my eyes flutter shut of their own volition. The scent that is uniquely Vanni, the sound of the waves—they surround me, lulling me into a temporary peace. I'm being pulled toward him much like the current gets pulled out to sea. And it feels just as inevitable.

My eyes open.

"I did not run."

I look into his eyes, and a single word courses through my head, my entire being.

Death.

The word so little belongs in this moment, it feels as if someone else planted it there. I know better. Although Amma has never had such visions, my mother did many times. It is a trait of some Garra. Only those with the blood of Athea in them, and who have also been properly trained and truly claim the title of Garra, can even hope to achieve such visions.

Amma says Athea had one before she supposedly broke the Kingdom of Meria.

A noblewoman named Lady Edina visited the healer to ask for a love potion to make King Onry II fall in love with her. Athea made it, though none know if she did so despite her vision of a broken kingdom, or as some speculate, because of it.

The potion worked, the king forsaking his betrothed for Lady Edina. Years later when King Onry chose a successor from his twins sons, the older son by mere minutes became enraged, leaving d'Almerita for the untamed Highlands to the east. The church later claimed the kingdom's split was punishment against Onry for forsaking his vows. They blamed Athea for her role, her ancestors forever cast into the shadows.

I attempt to give shape to this vision but cannot. It is instead more like a feeling of certainty that Vanni will deal a fatal blow, though when or against whom, I do not know.

I shake away the thought.

"I know why you left," he says, and the moment is gone, replaced by one I wish would never end.

"Aye?" I tease as Vanni closes the space between us.

"I will not hurt you, Aedre. Or betray you."

"Mayhap not apurpose, but you are not long for Murwood End."

A fact I no longer care to dwell on even as he acknowledges my words by not refuting them. Instead, he leans down toward me. More than a kiss, this is the culmination of the longing, the desire that has drawn us together from the start. And as his tongue prompts my lips to open, I give over gladly.

Who needs to breathe when such a man kisses you in this way?

Not gentle, like the way he holds my hand. Not deferential, as he was in the forge with my family. Not gentlemanly, as he appeared in the tavern that first day.

Nay, he kisses like a different kind of man all together. The one who can knock another warrior's sword from his hand with three strikes. Who bested Agnar after already fighting three others and threatened an Elderman with words none but he can speak.

When he lets go of my hands to pull me closer, I grasp Vanni's wide shoulders out of necessity, my legs weak with pleasure. The quick flicks of his tongue become deft strokes, ones that tell me what I've suspected.

He has kissed many a maid before, maybe one in every town he visits. And likely more so at court. For Vanni's kiss is adamant and strong and skillful, every bit what I'd expect from a man such as he.

When he groans against my lips, the thought of bringing him the same measure of pleasure emboldens me. Reminds me of all the ways I've learned to please a man, starting with how to kiss a man like Vanni.

Matching every touch, every thrust, of his tongue, I'm pulled deeper and deeper under until I can bear it no longer.

Stepping away, I attempt to slow the beating of my heart. I may be inexperienced, but I know there was an unusual power in our kiss. A deeper sense of connection.

"I thought," my words stumble over each other, "I thought if I did not pull away, I might not ever do so."

Vanni lets out a breath, his hands raking through the dark, thick hair I burn to touch.

"I should not have kissed you."

Staring at his lips, I violently disagree.

"Aye, you should have. I willed it so."

Today, last eve, the day before . . . every moment since I first saw him.

"As you said, I am not long for Murwood End."

He's telling me nothing I don't already know. It is plain enough to us both this is but a temporary arrangement.

"I've guarded the hearts of many a maid," I say, braver than I feel. "And will do so with my own."

From the look in his eyes, it's obvious he doesn't believe me. Nor should he.

"Your heart needs no such guarding."

Danger.

Death.

The strange pulse of knowledge comes to me again, the feeling much stronger this time.

What is my intuition trying to tell me? That he is dangerous to me? To someone else? Maybe Father Beald.

Or Kipp?

Nay, he said he would not force him, and I know Vanni to

be an honorable man. Even now, though I know he wishes to kiss me again, he waits for me to sort through my complicated emotions.

If I believed a Garra who'd never been in love herself was a fraud, this one, who is unable to protect her own heart, is even more so.

Love healer, indeed.

CHAPTER EIGHTEEN

VANNI

*T*his time, Aedre didn't run away.
 I did.

After that kiss . . .

That kiss.

Though I did not touch her again, every part of me wished it were otherwise. When we finally sat, I moved closer to her on the stone. And when she reached for my new sword, the one her father forged, I used the moment to brush my fingers across hers.

Except I don't want to simply kiss Lady Aedre. I want to consume, and be consumed by, her. When we're not together, I'm thinking of her, curious about what she's doing or who she's healing. I'm imagining her swinging the double-edged hammer she clearly knows how to wield. I'm sitting inside the inn listening but not really hearing my companions.

Thomas raises his voice, arguing with my squire, Christopher, over the merits of Voyager fishing nets and how they differ from those in the south.

But I care not about fishing nets. Or anything, really, save Master Aldwine's return.

And, of course, Aedre.

"You've not eaten yet," Thomas says to me, apparently finished with the good-natured disagreement.

In answer, I take a piece of fish and stuff it into my mouth.

"I spent the afternoon at the docks." Thomas smiles at the serving maid passing by. "And heard a rumor about the Queen of Edingham."

I eat, suddenly hungry after that one bite, as the innkeeper's daughter, a now-familiar serving maid, moves past us again. On many of our journeys we are hosted by noblemen. At other times, we stay in abbeys. But Sailor's Inn has fast become a favorite, despite my typical distaste for inns. With the exception of that first day, none have challenged us, and some appear to have forgotten there are strangers among them. Every day fewer and fewer patrons look our way.

"Celebrating the demise of Meria's lost heir already?" I ask.

Though the news must have traveled to Edingham by now, it's premature for it to have reached Murwood.

"Nay, though no doubt they'll do so soon enough. Some say Queen Cettina's sister has returned to court."

Salvi and I look at Thomas, both of us surprised.

"So Lord Whitley has finally found a home for his ambition?" Salvi asks.

The knight has served me well these past years, and there are none I rather wish to have by my side than he. Unlike Thomas, he is more reticent with his words.

"More like the queen's sister has found a way to get into her good graces."

An interesting development, if it is, indeed, true.

Though second-born, Cettina inherited her father's crown when he died the year after her older sister, Lady Hilla, was disinherited and banished. Rumor has it Lady Hilla had an affair with an especially unsuitable man, although none know the truth of it. Some say aye, and others nay. But all agree that when her father, the king, learned of the accusations, the man in question was swiftly beheaded, Lady Hilla and her husband exiled. Said husband, Lord Whitley, still rages over the incident.

"Either way, she and Whitley are back at Breywood Castle, if the stories are true."

I consider how this may affect our current state of affairs.

"If stories of Whitley's ambition and greed are true, he will undoubtedly make a play for his wife to reclaim the crown." I take a swig of ale.

"Perhaps Meria won't be alone in her misery?" Thomas speculates.

I've come to the same conclusion.

"This is good news for us," I agree. "But Edingham's instability does little to solve our own problems."

The group falls silent until my squire speaks up.

"What will we do if he doesn't come with us?"

The others look at Christopher and then back at me.

"The king refused to name another heir, but if Aldwine refuses us—" my teeth grind at the possibility, "—the king will have to name another."

"Who?" Thomas asks.

I have my suspicions, but none are fact, so I will keep such thoughts to myself.

"It matters not. If the church backs Hinton, along with those who support him already, 'twill ensure a long and bloody path forward for Meria."

Our uneasy silence is broken by the sound of the inn door swinging open.

"The Artemis has returned," someone calls excitedly.

My hand drops back to the table, my mug hitting it with a thud.

Thomas and I exchange a glance before we both shift our attention back to the door. More watching and waiting. After more than one of the Sailor's Inn patrons leaves, we have our answer.

Voyagers are known to put into port, even at night, rather than anchoring.

Without saying a word, I nod, and the four of us stand at once. Because of Aedre, I am not worried about gaining an audience with him immediately. Even so, I would glimpse the man that may yet be king of Meria.

A crowd has already gathered along the wharf.

"There's hardly any moonlight," Salvi says, lifting the lantern he'd taken with him. "Do you know any ship captains who would put in on a night such as this?"

"Madness," Thomas mutters.

I tend to agree. But Voyagers are also known for their skill in the water. The tragedy that cost Meria so dearly would likely not have happened in Murwood End.

"Can you see the ship?" Christopher asks as we approach.

"Nay." The crowd has grown, presumably for first pick of the furs Aldwine's men have traded for oil. A curious custom, the makeshift port-side fair, but one that has become familiar. Despite the dark, townsfolk have descended on the Artemis, and we can see nothing of note for some time.

Eventually establishing a position with a vantage point that allows us to see the Voyagers as they make their way ashore, we blend into the crowd. Nothing marks us as king's men, for we've learned dressing the part makes the townspeople hosts uneasy.

"Look there," Thomas says, but I've already noticed him. Something about Master Aldwine draws the eye toward him, and it is not just his height. I step closer for a better look at the man.

Goods are tossed ashore, Aldwine pointing and shouting, though I can't hear his words. It is just as well. I can see the men look to him for their orders. I can see that he holds his head high. Though I hear nothing, I see everything. The rumors are all true.

The king insists Kipp Aldwine has grown to be a man who can be trusted with his crown and the ruling of Meria. And though it is not for me to question Galfrid's judgment, I am most curious about his bastard son.

"They say he can swing a sword while carrying ten men on his back, and now that I see him, I can understand how such a thing is possible," Christopher says.

I shake my head. "If I told you he pushed the ship into port, swimming behind it in the water, you'd believe that too?"

The others laugh.

"He believed me when I told him you drank the blood of your enemies for strength," Thomas adds. "So aye, he would . . . ow." Thomas rubs his arm, looking at Christopher as if he'd dearly love to strike him back. But I gesture for them to quiet their talk.

"He disembarks."

Leaving the others behind with a shouted order that I cannot hear, Aldwine makes his way through the crowd. Slaps on the back and words of welcome tell me that he is well-liked.

By Aedre too.

The twinge of jealousy is not new. She speaks of him as a god. No ill words ever leave her mouth where Aldwine is concerned. And though she's told me more than once that he is as a brother to her, now, seeing the man, I wonder how such a thing is possible. Even I can see another rumor of him is indeed true.

Though his father is also a good-looking man, Aldwine is more handsome by far. I've heard many stories of Aldwine's mother, even from the king himself. If he did love her, as he claimed, perhaps her beauty played a role?

As he approaches our spot, I imagine Aldwine and Aedre together and then immediately push the vile thought away, replacing it with another more pleasant one. Of Aedre in my arms, kissing me with abandon, responding to each stroke of my tongue with one of her own.

"Glaring at the man will not bring him around to our cause," Thomas says beside me.

I turn my head toward him, away from the king's son.

"I was not glaring."

My voice is thick with jealousy.

Thomas clears his throat.

"I may have been glaring," I admit. And Thomas knows why. I've told him about Aedre's promise to set up a meeting with Aldwine. He is intelligent enough to surmise the rest.

"God willing, he will be the next king of Meria." He lowers his voice. "Remember your purpose here, Vanni."

I look back at Aldwine as he makes his way through the crowd.

Never in all the years I've served Galfrid have I given a reason for my loyalty, my motives, to be questioned. And as much as I wish to lash out at Thomas, to refute his words, it would be foolish to do so.

I *had* forgotten our purpose, if only momentarily. I'm not here to steal kisses from Aedre, however pleasing it would be. My purpose is to speak with that man, the one being feted by his people. The one Aedre and her family do not believe will return with us.

My *duty* is to convince him otherwise.

CHAPTER NINETEEN
AEDRE

*T*hough just on the edge of the village, the walk to Nord Manor takes a bit of time and effort. Built on a massive rock island, the base of which becomes submerged at high tide, it is an impregnable and impressive structure. As I walk the long path leading to it, the low tide allowing me to pass, my mind turns over and over again, as it has since yesterday. So many questions invade my thoughts. I have a clear answer to only one.

Should I have kissed Lord Vanni d'Abella, Curia Commander to the King of Meria?

The answer is a resounding yes.

Had I gone a lifetime without such a kiss, I would never have understood the power of love, of desire—why people are willing to drink any concoction, recite any spell, for such a feeling.

Of course, I am not *in love* with Vanni. But he does invoke something in me I'd never experienced or understood before. Not really.

While some imagine themselves at court, surrounded by elaborate gowns and glorious luxuries, I've not once wished for such things. My grandmother has ensured I wish only to be surrounded by love. By my family. Someday, perhaps, that family will grow and I will take a husband.

Unfortunately, Vanni could never be that man. He is King Galfrid's man through and through.

I come to the gatehouse after an uphill climb. A small tower with its circled stone wall encompassing the keep within its courtyard greets me, and I wave up at the guard. Though I can't see his face from here, the portcullis is opened. Surrounded by water, this small island accessible only during low tide took years to build but is considered the crowning glory of Murwood End, much to the consternation of Lord Bailor, the highest ranking noble here. Kipp's father, Sir Nicholas, was knighted on the battlefield but held no other title. A mercenary, he'd saved a lifetime's worth of gold to make Nord Manor possible.

A good man, Nicholas Aldwine had left this manor, which would be considered a castle by some, as well as his legacy, to Kipp, whom he'd accepted as his son.

Kipp would never leave it, most especially not to return to a man he despises. But I made a promise to Vanni and intend to keep it. Even if it hastens Vanni's departure from Murwood End.

I refuse to regret that kiss.

"Good day, Lady Aedre," Kipp's steward, one of just a handful of servants at Nord, greets me as he opens the door.

"Good day." I walk inside and spot him immediately.

Kipp is a difficult man to miss. As always, he is dressed simply. Braies and a linen tunic, given the warm temperature. And yet, he's a tall, broad man, and there's a regal quality to him that must have been passed to him in Galfrid's blood. It is a silly thought, but difficult to dismiss.

I could very much imagine him on the throne.

"Aedre? I'd have come to see you," he says, leaping up

from his chair. Unlike at Lord Bailor's home, Anbarth Castle, there is no dais or special seat for Kipp. As he says often, he is neither a great lord or even a knight but a Voyager and the son of a mercenary.

"Today? Tomorrow? A sennight from now?"

He wraps his arms around me and I squeeze back, grateful for his return.

"I'd have come—" he releases me, laughing, "—eventually."

There are few in the hall. I raise my hand to greet the men who hardly leave Kipp's side, a group of twelve fellow Voyagers as loyal to Kipp as if he were their lord.

They say Nord Manor is akin to a monastery for the abundance of unmarried men and lack of women. With two very obvious differences . . . they're neither religious or celibate.

"Not soon enough." I nod away from the hall. "I'd speak to you privately."

The words have barely left my mouth before Kipp starts striding toward the entranceway whence I just emerged.

A small solar just up the stairs is by far the most spectacular chamber in the entire manor. It boasts large windows open to the sea beyond.

"Something's troubling you?" he asks as he settles into his chair.

I sit across from him in a high back, velvet-lined chair. The upholstery is brightly colored, much like the tapestries that hang on the walls—Kipp's mother's attempt to lighten the long, dark days here in the north.

"Have you spoken to anyone since returning?"

"Last eve when we made port, aye."

"Then you've heard we have visitors?"

A visit by the king's men would likely be one of the first pieces of news Kipp learned of upon his return. Not because everyone knows his secret, for they don't, but because it is the most significant thing to have happened in Murwood End of late.

"Aye."

Suspicious now, Kipp's jaw ticks as it is wont to do.

"What were you told of them?"

Crossing his arms, Kipp leans back in his chair, legs outstretched. I will not tell him, for his sorrow at his adoptive father's passing has not yet abated, but Kipp reminds me very much of him at this moment. In this position.

"There are four of them. Their leader is King Galfrid's commander."

I nod.

"The commander has bested many men, including Agnar, since he arrived less than a sennight ago."

"You are well-informed."

He frowns. "Though not as well-informed as you, I presume?"

If only Kipp knew the whole truth. I debate telling him, as I usually share everything with him, more so even than Amma. But this feels . . . different.

Something in my expression must put him on alert, for he leans forward, no longer relaxed at all. Knowing Kipp as I do, I blurt out the news so as not to delay the inevitable.

"The prince is dead. Drowned in a shipwreck. They're here to convince you to return with them."

I wait for him to grasp the full import of my words.

"Return with them . . ."

Bracing for his reaction, I say, "To be named as King Galfrid's successor."

Eyes wide, Kipp jumps from his seat, curses tumbling from his mouth.

I stand, look out to the sea, and wait for him to calm.

"Whoreson. He thinks I would do such a thing?" I do not answer, knowing he is speaking to himself. "After all these years . . . he only cares to remember who I am now that his precious son is dead. God rest his soul."

Kipp is not a cruel man, so I'm thankful he added the last bit, though the sentiment surprises me too. He has never been a religious man.

He turns to me. "No," he says adamantly. "*Never.*"

Sighing, I push the shutters open wider. From up here, we can hear the sound of waves crashing against the rocks below. Who could live apart from the sea? I could not dream of it.

"There is more I should tell you."

Kipp's shoulders rise and fall, his anger understandable. If Prince Matteo had not died in that shipwreck, Kipp would not be in the line of succession at all. And I know he's never gotten over his anger at his true father—the man who seduced his mother, then exiled her from court.

Still . . .

"I have gotten to know the commander."

Kipp turns to me, eyes narrowed.

"I told him I would gain an audience with you."

Kipp is already shaking his head.

"Please, 'tis just an audience. I already warned him you will not go back to Castle d'Almerita. For me?"

Covering his face with his hands, Kipp rubs his eyes in annoyance.

"I'm sorry, Kipp. Please do this. I promised him."

He folds his hands together, aggrieved, and asks the one question I cannot answer. Not unless I plan to tell him all.

"Why would you promise such a thing?"

Kipp is angry with me, something that has only happened once before. I snuck onto his ship once as a young girl of ten and two, Kipp being five years older. He found me after less than a half day at sea and promptly turned back to the shore, refusing to speak to me until we spotted land. We laugh at the incident now, yet it is still a matter of debate between us. Young boys voyaged, and yet I was not allowed. He argued it was my father's wish, but even so, the inequality rankled.

"I . . ."

Part of me wishes to lie. But despite that one occasion when he sided with his father over me, Kipp has always been my staunch defender. And I know down to my bones he would never, ever lie to me.

So neither can I lie to him.

How do I say this? Or, more precisely, what do I say? That Vanni has already launched over the walls I spent years putting up?

"Aedre?"

I swallow.

"If he has dishonored you . . ."

"Nay, he has not. Do you think so little of me that you'd believe I would beg a favor for a man who has done me wrong? Vanni is all you've been told, and more. He's honorable and kind, and has done nothing to incur your wrath." I add quickly, "Certainly nothing involving me."

For he is, after all, King Galfrid's man. And that ensures Kipp will never call him a friend.

"Tell me."

We've discussed plenty of sensitive topics before—the sort of things some people dare never speak of aloud. My training as a Garra ensures I'm not overly sensitive. And yet, I feel my cheeks warm.

"He kissed me."

Kipp waits as if to say, *Is that all?*

"'Twas nothing like the others. Not even a bit."

Kipp knows about my insecurities—my fear that I'm a hypocrite for helping others with love and desire when I've never experienced much of it myself. And so he softens, if just a little.

"I'm glad for it, Aedre. Truly, I am. But of all the men you could choose . . ."

"But I did not. Not truly. He is a noble, nearly a royal. And yet, when we met, I could not deny my attraction to him."

Kipp seems to have calmed, though I worry about what that means. He has to agree to meet with Vanni, even if just to tell him no himself.

"So what happened?"

What indeed?

"'Tis a story for another time, but for various reasons, I have found myself in his presence almost every day since he arrived."

Kipp makes a sound in the back of his throat. "Reasons? Ones contrived by you? Or by the very noble commander?"

I cross my arms. "Maybe by Vanni. But that matters not."

"Ha! It matters, my dear Aedre. He seduced you."

Seduced me to gain an audience with Kipp. I've considered as such, and even if I do not truly believe it, I'm practical enough to recognize there might be some truth to Kipp's words.

"He could not have known. I only admitted to knowing your secret after he revealed his true purpose."

Kipp is not convinced.

"Did he know we were friends?"

I think back. "Not at first."

"But when he learned of it?"

In truth, I cannot guess at Vanni's true intentions. I don't know the man that well. But I do know one thing. "He desired me from the start." I add in a small voice, "And I him."

Before Kipp can answer, I tell him about the incident with Father Beald. Angry again, but this time for a very different reason, Kipp clearly wishes to pick up where Vanni left off. Though he might actually do the man harm, if his expression is any indication.

"He's banished him, of sorts," I quickly explain, and there's a slight softening in Kipp. Very slight.

"So he used his influence to help you. Still, I suspect his motivations."

"Ugh." He can be so maddening. So very stubborn.

"Come, eat with us. 'Tis enough talk of Galfrid's man."

I try to argue, but he tugs my hand as a brother would.

"Will you see him?"

Kipp doesn't answer but fairly pulls me from the solar instead.

Maddening.

The whole lot of them.

CHAPTER TWENTY
VANNI

"*B*e patient," I insist. "She will gain us an audience."

Christopher looks behind me as we finish our practice session. My men are impatient for news about Aldwine, especially now that he's returned, and there's no better way to pass the time than in training. Accepting challenges, honing our skills for the dark days ahead. Whether or not we return with the bastard king, I fear we will be called upon to fight for Meria's future.

The widening of Christopher's eyes tells me who stands at the entrance to the inn's courtyard. "It seems your faith in her was not misplaced," he says, leaving. "She is here."

I gasp like an untrained lad when I turn to see her. Aedre has always dressed simply before, but not this eve.

She stands before me in a deep blue velvet gown lined in gold, her hair pulled away from her face with a simple gold circlet.

In a flash, I find myself envisioning her by my side at court.

None would rival her.

It takes me a moment to realize she's staring back with an equal degree of intensity.

I walk toward her, feeling my body react to her presence. To her admiration. Aedre's lips open, just slightly, her eyes trained on my bare chest.

"Pardon me, Lady Aedre." I make for the wooden quintain and grab my shirt.

"You need not . . ."

Sheathing my sword, I pause for her to finish.

". . . beg my pardon, for intruding on your practice."

Smiling, I take a step toward her.

"I thought you might say I need not put this on." I gesture to the shirt, which I then pull over my head.

She gives me a skeptical, weighing look—the same way she regarded me that very first day, when we met along the quay.

"I've seen men without their shirts on before."

I glance around. Since we are alone, I decide to test her bravado.

"Aye?"

Another step toward her.

"Aye," she says more firmly, so close now her lavender scent reaches me. I breathe it in, aching to reach out and touch her.

Closing the remaining distance between us, I pray Aedre will not be offended by my words. "And have you allowed many of those men you've seen as such to kiss you?" I search her eyes for the truth. "To taste your sweetness as I have done? To awaken something inside"—I venture a guess now —"that you've never felt before?"

A guess based on my own experience.

This . . . thing between us is unique. Even as I rebel against it, knowing my duty requires me to leave her—

knowing also she would never wish to come to court with me—I cannot deny that.

"You are bold, sir."

"And would be bolder still, would you allow it."

"Is that so?"

It should not be so at all. But her eyes burn in a way that invites me to speak.

"Aye."

No additional words are spoken, for none are needed. But Aedre is a lady, and a virgin. The code of honor dictates that we cannot lie together.

And still, I find myself saying, "Were circumstances different, I would not have put it back on but would have instead taken your hand and laid it on my chest. I'd have kissed you already, Aedre, and shown you just how dearly I wish you would touch all of me."

A final step toward her.

I dare not move any closer.

I'm sure she will slap me at any moment. But this is no simpering maid. This woman has held a knife to my throat. Her manner of speaking is so bold, so brazen, it never fails to surprise me.

"I came here for a reason." Her voice, thick, is not unaffected.

I should care very much about her reasons for seeking me out, especially given her connection to Aldwine, but first, I'd know one thing.

"Do you wish to touch me, Aedre?"

Though we are alone at the moment, the courtyard having cleared as all who practiced or watched headed indoors for supper, such a fact could change at any time. Even so, I cannot help myself.

"Aedre?"

Before I can help myself, I reach for her. Aedre does not

recoil from my hand, instead allowing it to graze her cheek. It feels as her gown looks, so soft and smooth.

Her eyes close, thick dark lashes against her cheeks. Part of me aches to forget everything and taste her again. Yet the sight of my rough hand against her flesh is reminder enough of who I am and why I am here. I am a warrior, a commander. My hands were made for fighting, not loving.

I pull my hand away. "You did not come here to be mauled by me."

"Hmm," she murmurs. "Mayhap I did."

Her words do not help, even though I asked for such torture. Another vision, this time of me hauling her up against the stone building behind her, using it as leverage as I hold her at my waist, sinking into her, claiming her . . .

Groaning, I step back, attempting to regain control.

"You said you've come for a purpose, and 'twas likely not to be mistreated by me."

"Nay," she says adamantly, "you would never do that."

I look into her eyes.

"Nay, I would not."

After a moment, one no words could sufficiently fill, she says, "I came to tell you that I've seen Kipp."

Before I can respond, she rushes to add, "Lord Bailor is hosting a feast in honor of the men's safe return. I am on my way there now."

Ah, the reason for her gown.

"Kipp will be there. And he will receive you on the morrow."

I want to wrap my arms around her.

"I'd have come here sooner, but when I returned home, Father was not feeling well. So I dressed, hoping . . . hoping you might escort me there."

"To Anbarth Castle?"

Aedre nods. "My father and I were invited, but perhaps you could escort me instead?"

"Would it be proper, for me to escort you, alone? Your father . . ."

"Trusts that I can judge a man's character well. He knows that I am here, asking you this very question."

"Such strange customs." I stop myself. "Nay, not strange. Different than my own. Thank you." I'm not sure what I'm thanking her for, exactly, arranging our meeting with Kipp or inviting me to spend the eve with her. It will likely be our last chance to do so. Once we meet with Kipp, there will be no further reason to stay. Galfrid needs us, needs me, in the south.

The thought is a heavy one, but I won't allow it to ruin our night.

"You are an angel."

I would hug her. Kiss her.

I would make her mine, if I could.

"Come into the inn while I prepare. I'll do so quickly."

"Vanni." She lays a hand on my shoulder before I can walk away, staying me. I resist the urge to grasp it. To kiss it. To touch the inside of her wrist with my lips, my tongue . . .

"Do not thank me yet. You may have an audience, but I do not believe you will have your king."

I don't let her words affect the gleeful mood I suddenly find myself in.

"We shall see." I smile. "I can be quite persuasive."

CHAPTER TWENTY-ONE
AEDRE

*W*hen Kipp agreed to meet Vanni on the morrow, my victory felt hollow. He only agreed for my sake, and I know his answer will not be to Vanni's liking. My heart felt heavy too, burdened by the knowledge that Vanni will leave after their meeting.

By the time I reached home to news of Lord Bailor's invitation, Amma knew something was wrong. The blasted tears would not stop flowing.

Holding me to her chest, she stroked my hair as if I were a young girl. She did not chastise me, although I would have understood if she had. I've known Vanni for less than a sennight. But Amma reminded me of the heart's wayward notions.

"There is nothing as unpredictable as love," she'd said.

My stupid heart chose a man that I cannot have.

When father returned home with the invitation from Lord Bailor and said he felt too weary to attend, Amma and I exchanged a glance. I knew without asking that we shared the same thought—a surprising turnaround given her attitude the first time we discussed Lord d'Abella.

"Mayhap the commander could escort me?"

Amma was quick to add, "He is an honorable man, the king's commander. I think 'tis a fine idea."

Father attempted to argue, but Amma didn't make it easy on him.

"Who should she ask instead? Agnar? He covets the child still, and you know it well, Dal."

Child.

I tried not to grin at Amma's words.

"Agnar would not dishonor her," he says hesitantly. "We know little of this commander."

"'Tis not true, Father. I know the king trusts him with his life. And that he is loyal and respectful. I've learned from you well and would not risk myself for any man."

It had taken a bit more convincing, but he'd relented in the end. As Vanni said, our ways are not so rigid here. The people of Murwood End pride themselves on flaunting the conventions of the south and east. Of the very courts they fled from.

As I wait for him in front of the inn, watching the fishermen unload and the final flurry of activity of the day, I think of myself a few days hence, watching the same scene knowing Vanni will not emerge from the inn behind me. He will be long gone, a distant memory.

I've healed so many of the ache of lost love, but can I heal myself?

"Apologies if I kept you waiting overly long, my lady."

I turn, amazed at how quickly he's transformed. Hair still damp, he is otherwise impeccably put together, the king's seal emblazoned on his tunic. This is the commander I met that first day. It's a much-needed reminder that he isn't a Voyager, even if he and his men have taken to dressing like our people.

"You look . . ."

Commanding. Magnificent. Handsome.

". . . like a king's man."

Instead of being offended, he bows ever so formally.

"A king's man at your service, my lady. I shall not abuse the duty your father has entrusted me with as your escort."

I'm not disappointed by his words. I thought only of spending time with him, being near him. Any further intimacies would only make our future separation that much harder. And yet, the thought of kissing him again . . .

The sound of hoofbeats coming from the courtyard behind us distracts me. One of Vanni's men—his squire, I believe—leads a massive warhorse toward us.

I shake my head.

"Nay. I do not ride."

Vanni seems surprised by that. "I know you've few horses here, but surely you've ridden one before?"

"There is no building in Murwood End I cannot walk to, so nay, I've never ridden a horse before. Most of our people travel by sea, and no visitors have ever offered to take me for a ride. Nor would have I accepted if they had done so."

"Dex will not harm you."

He takes my hand and leads me to him, placing it on the horse's mane. His hair is rough yet surprisingly smooth despite it. Such a large animal. Yet he has gentle, patient eyes. A calm comes over me as I stroke him, the horse's energy easily identifiable as peaceful.

"Shall I bring him back to the stables, lord?"

Vanni looks from his squire to me, the question plain in his eyes. While I'd prefer to walk, mayhap this is a night for adventure.

"I would ride with you?"

"Aye."

Vanni will keep me safe. So I nod.

He mounts easily despite the horse's size.

"Give me your hand," he commands. "Hike up your gown and put your foot there." He points to the stirrup. "Toss the other one over Dex's side."

I do as he says and, as easily as if I were a child, he pulls me up in front of him. Settling in, I rearrange my gown, but my gaze finds the ground. It is so far down.

"I'm scared," I admit, whispering so his squire does not hear me.

Vanni leans forward, his breath tickling my exposed ear.

"There is no need to be afraid when you are with me, Aedre."

Though I know his promise only extends to this eve, I can't help wishing it meant something more. Something *longer*.

Wrapping one arm around my waist, he takes the reins from his squire with the other.

I jolt a little as we begin to move forward, but he tightens his grip.

"I'll not let go," he says in my ear, sending a very different jolt through me.

The sight of a horse making its way along the quay is not so unusual as to garner much attention, yet everyone who sees us stares. Perhaps it's Vanni they're looking at—I know I won't be able to stop staring at him all night—or it may be the sight of us together that interests them so.

"How do you feel?" he asks.

More secure than I should.

"Odd," I admit. Father and Amma will be amused to hear about this. I'd never expected to ride a horse. Nor had I ever given thought to leaving Murwood End. I won't, of course, but riding with Vanni, my back pressed to his front, I'm struck by the image of us riding off together. Going somewhere else.

Desire truly does make a person act insensibly.

"Dex is more accustomed to battle than he is to bearing two riders, but he's doing well."

When I look back at Vanni, his face so very close, I find it difficult to reconcile this man with the one who sheltered with me in the sea cave. This is the nobleman I first met.

"You really are the king's commander."

His smile is so easily given I cannot help but return it. "I am."

"'Tis impressive for a man your age?"

So as not to strain my neck, I look out toward the water, but I can still see Vanni's profile. I can feel him behind me.

"I am the youngest in Meria's history."

He does not say it as a boast, but more just a simple fact.

"Were you begrudged over the title?"

"Perhaps by some. When my parents died, the king ordered me to be trained by a man named Albertus, who also trained his son." He pauses, then adds, "He and Aldwine's father served in the same company."

"You were trained by a mercenary?"

"Aye, and one of the best. Have you heard of the Legion of Ash?"

"Of course."

Kipp's father was a member. As was this man, Albertus, it seems.

"Kipp says they disbanded many years ago."

At his silence, I turn toward him. "Have they not?"

There's a sadness in Vanni I'm not accustomed to seeing.

"Aye, they have. Some have died, others joined different companies. There are whispers of a secret order of its former members, but I've not seen evidence of one. After Albertus died, Matteo and I heard less and less of them."

"You were close with Prince Matteo, then?"

"I was. I remember one day during pell training Albertus had us practicing for so long my eyes began to sting.

Matteo later asked him why we'd not been given a break that day."

His face, suddenly so unguarded, takes me aback.

"Instead of answering, Albertus continued the session, well into the night. Lanterns surrounded us, the men who held them more amused than us. It was the last time either Matteo or I asked Albertus to end a training session."

His sad smile is so bittersweet my shoulders sag in sorrow for him.

"I am sorry, Vanni."

Unable to bear the pain on his face, I turn back, sorry I mistreated him when we first met. Our ways are, indeed, different. His arm tightens around me as Anbarth Castle comes into view. Built by Lord Bailor's ancestors, among the first in Murwood, it is on the opposite end of the village from Nord, just beyond the Cliffs of Murh, which we ride alongside now.

Built atop the highest cliff, encircled by a stone wall and small inner courtyard, the castle itself is eclipsed by its surroundings.

The castle stands tall before us. As a blacksmith's daughter, I should have little cause to visit such a place. But Lord Bailor is not a typical nobleman. Most often, we do not even think of him as one at all, but as a Voyager who happens to live in a grand place.

Amma said he learned from the mistakes of his grandfather, who attempted to lead the people of Murwood, even naming himself king. For his efforts, he was pushed off the very cliff we pass now. A stone marker reminds those who pass it of Voyagers' intolerance of being ruled by others. Bailor's father learned the lesson well, quietly taking the inheritance of Anbarth but never attempting to extend his claim beyond its walls.

On a whim, I put my hand over Vanni's grip on my waist.

To comfort him about his loss. Or at least, that is the reason I give myself for doing it. In response, Vanni slows Dex to near stopping. And then I feel him leaning in close to my ear once again.

"I promised to give you safe escort, and will do so. Just so that we are clear, my lady, it is the only reason I haven't kissed you yet."

His rough knuckles shift under my fingers, but they do not push me away. If I turn my head even the slightest, his lips will touch mine.

You will not see him again after tomorrow. Tonight, maybe one other night, and then Vanni will be gone.

And yet, I'm about to turn toward him anyway when someone calls to us from behind. Vanni dismounts and holds a hand up to me. Reluctantly, I let him assist me. Feet firmly on the ground, I'm about to walk around Dex to greet the cobbler, who's approaching us from a distance with a wide grin, when Vanni stops me.

"But I may do so yet this eve, when my escort duties are over, Lady Aedre," he says with a wink.

CHAPTER TWENTY-TWO
VANNI

I spot him immediately. Even if I hadn't seen him last night, I would have known him on sight. He stands taller than any of the others, both in height and in bearing. His high cheekbones give him the look of Galfrid.

Apparently Kipp sees us as well. Mid-conversation, he turns from his companions and makes his way toward us. He's at the back of the great hall, though, and we've just entered it. Judging by the people who keep stopping him for a word or a greeting, it may take him a while to reach us. Having greeted our host and hostess, Aedre and I walk toward the gathering crowd, which is perhaps fifty or a bit more in number.

"They are unaccustomed to seeing someone of your ilk here," she whispers.

Forgetting Aldwine for a moment, I shake my head. "They are looking at you, Aedre. Not me."

From what I've learned of Aedre thus far, she is very much in tune with others' feelings. Their distress. Their interests. Their passions. But not so much her own.

I would change that.

"He's coming toward us," Aedre says.

"I see him."

A serving girl approaches us with two goblets of wine, which we take with our thanks.

I'm desperately going to need some wine after that ride. For as long as I live, I will remember the feeling of Aedre's backside pressing against me. Of the way she laid her hand over mine, as if to tell me I wasn't alone. That she felt and saw my pain.

"Aedre?"

It's both a question and a warning. Aldwine glares at me as he would an enemy.

"'Tis good to see you again so soon, Kipp," she says. "May I introduce my escort, Lord Vanni d'Abella?"

"Escort?" he spits out.

Taking exception to his tone, I interject with, "My intentions are honorable, I can assure you."

I reach out my hand, but Aldwine does not take it.

He is every bit a Voyager. And a warrior, too. Though I suspect the rumors of unprovoked attacks by such men are nothing more than rumors, I understand why so many believe them to be true.

"Your *intention* is to gain an audience with me."

His tone is hard. Unforgiving.

I look at Aedre and realize what he's said to her. He believes I used her to get to him.

"You do not believe that?" I address her, not him.

Aedre takes a sip of wine but does not answer. I wait, ignoring Aldwine.

"Aedre?"

She blinks and lowers her goblet.

"I do not believe that."

Though she says the words, I can tell the possibility bothers her. And although one of the reasons I originally sought an audience with her was to gain access to Kipp, my feelings for her are very real.

"I cannot say the same," Aldwine bites out.

So it seems I've complicated my mission here by having grown close to a woman he cares for.

"I've no argument with you, Master Aldwine," I say, mostly sincere.

His lips flatten. "Again, I cannot say the same."

"Kipp."

Her scolding tone amuses me. Aedre addresses the future king like she might a wayward child.

"You should not have brought him here," Kipp sneers. "If you needed escort, I could have provided it."

Aedre rolls her eyes. "By the time my father shared the invitation and his intent to stay home, there was little time to send for you."

"And yet you sent for *him*?"

If Aldwine were any other man in the world, I'd have a retort for that. Would likely already have challenged him.

But this is Galfrid's son.

"He is staying in the village. Besides, I've told you already, I trust him. So enough of this silliness. Please be kind."

I assume he will do no such thing, but at her words, Aldwine frowns, turns to me, and lifts the goblet in his hand.

"Good eve, then. We shall speak on the morrow. For Aedre."

Not quite a civil tone, but not combative either.

"No need to part ways so soon, Kipp," she says with a smile. "We will sit with you this eve."

His scowl is quick to return. "The hell you will."

I watch the exchange closely for any hint of flirting. There is none. They do speak to each other as a sister and brother might . . . and Kipp does not look at her the way a potential suitor would.

The way I myself probably do.

"We shall see," Aedre murmurs as Kipp wanders off.

I should be worried about Aldwine's impression of me, which is obviously bad, but my mind is fixed on Aedre. I need her to understand something.

"I did not cultivate a relationship with you because of your access to him."

As we talk, I move us toward the edge of the hall.

"You know that, Aedre, do you not?"

Her intelligent eyes look deep into my own.

"Is that what we have been doing these past days? Cultivating?"

She is as blunt as usual, so I honor her by speaking the same way.

"I don't know. 'Tis the most honest answer I can give you. I should have stayed away, but could not."

"You will be leaving soon."

A fact we both have known from the start.

"Aye. Which is why I should have stayed away." I lower my voice. "I'd not trifle with you, Aedre."

"I know. Let us enjoy this night. Tomorrow, you will meet with Kipp and then . . ."

And then, I will leave Murwood End. A heaviness in my chest reminds me of how little time we have remaining.

"I will not leave on the morrow," I assure her.

"But perhaps the day afterward?"

"Likely, aye."

She looks toward the center of the hall, where guests are beginning to sit at trestle tables lined up one after the other.

"'Tis enough."

I have no time to contemplate her words, to understand their meeting. A discussion at the entrance draws our attention. I see the Elderman and react immediately.

CHAPTER TWENTY-THREE
AEDRE

*V*anni makes toward the entrance just as I see Father Beald entering the hall. I'd hoped the noxious man had left Murwood End, never to be seen again. Unfortunately, Lord Bailor ushers him inside just as Vanni makes his way through the crowd.

I see him wait until the Elderman leaves our host, and then he descends. I cannot hear their words, but Vanni looks furious.

I rush forward to join them, wishing to avoid a scene.

"Shall I swim to Hempswood, then?"

Vanni's eyes blaze. He is not at all the man I just spoke with. This Vanni raises the hairs on my neck. He's angry, every bit as much as he was that day at Sailor's Inn.

"I care not if you commission a ship or find a mount to cross the damn Loigh Mountains."

Father Beald glances at me. And though their voices are low, half the occupants of the hall, Lord Bailor included, are watching us.

"I agreed not to return, not to leave Murwood immediately." His voice carries the confidence of a man with few enemies.

"You agreed to never find yourself within reach of her ever again."

The sharp edge of Vanni's tone is not lost on those around us.

"Either make yourself scarce or consider hard the consequences we discussed."

A new voice adds, "Can you not discern you're unwanted here?"

Kipp.

If Father Beald holds Vanni and I in disregard, he has even less respect for Kipp. The two have fought many times before, the Elderman's threats hanging over us both. I have often wondered what he would think of Kipp's true parentage.

"Ah, the great Voyager has returned. How many men did you kill on this journey, Master Aldwine?"

"And how many of Murwood's people have you converted to your cause, Father Beald?"

Vanni doesn't give him a chance to answer.

"Why are you here?" he presses.

Father Beald looks at me and then glances between Vanni and Kipp.

"It seems you have acquired not one but two protectors, Mistress Aedre. Learning from Edrys how to use your Garra skills to entrap a man?"

My hand rises before I can reconsider. The sound of my palm connecting with his cheek echoes in the hall, cutting through the sound of talking and laughter.

The Elderman's eyes widen as Lord Bailor steps in.

"I invited you out of courtesy, Father Beald. But I believe your welcome here has run its course."

My hand still stings, but I feel no remorse. Not even when his cheek turns pink where I struck it.

And then I see Vanni's face.

Knowing real terror for the first time in my life, I grab his hand and pull him away. The crowd parts for us, and we move to the far end of the hall near the kitchens.

"You cannot kill an Elderman," I say, knowing full well he may have done just that had we lingered. The look of pure fury on his face is only now lifting. Slightly. "He's gone," I say, watching Father Beald leave the hall.

His shoulders rising and falling, Vanni looks at me for the first time since I pulled him back here.

"I'm sorry, Aedre."

I pray to the very man Father Beald wields as his ultimate weapon.

Dear God, give me the strength to deal with all men.

"You need not apologize, Vanni. I appreciate you trying to protect me. But as you can see, I am not powerless to defend myself."

Kipp reaches us then.

"Let me see it." He grabs my hand. "Does it hurt?"

I pull away, give both of them a hard look, and then turn back toward the front of the hall. With the Elderman gone, I make my way toward Lord Bailor to apologize for my actions. While I'm not sorry for having slapped a man who suggested that Amma taught me how to whore for protection, I am sorry for having altered the celebratory mood of the evening.

But I will make it right if I must lead the singing and dancing myself.

Vanni and Kipp can glare at each other in the meantime. With luck, they will both still be standing when I return.

~

IN THE END, we did not sit with Kipp. After apologizing to Lord Bailor and his wife, I found Vanni in a conversation with one of Murwood's only other noblemen, a minor baron from Edingham who landed on our shores ten years earlier and never left. By the time the two finish talking, the only open seats remaining are in the back of the hall.

"You do not sit according to rank?" Vanni whispers as Bailor's steward guides us to the open seats.

Has he learned nothing from his time here?

"Rank means very little here. You forget I am but a black-smith's daughter. Would I be welcome at such a feast in d'Almerita?"

Vanni doesn't answer, which is just as well. I already know that I would not.

"Did you speak to Kipp after I left?"

We take our seats. The other occupants of the table eye Vanni suspiciously as we do so, but they are quick to return to their own conversation. Just as Vanni is quick to return to ours.

"If you consider a grunted 'Goddamn Elderman' a conversation, then aye."

We talk of the incident and of the differences between Murwood End and Meria. Vanni shares tales of his child-hood and training, and I tell him of Aloisa and others whom I've treated.

When the music begins after dinner, Vanni takes my hand and leads me to the center of the hall. And before I know it, he's spinning me around expertly, making me laugh harder than I ever have before. The man knows how to dance, a surprise given his profession.

"I spend much time at court," he explains, spinning me away from him and then back again.

"Do you attract much attention there?"

I already know that he does, but Vanni merely shrugs.

"How do you not have a court of noblewomen begging for you to marry them?"

"Did I say that I do not?"

I laugh, even though we both know he likely speaks the truth.

It feels as if my problems are lifted away, if only temporarily. The only weight I feel is that of Kipp's glaring eyes. Two songs later, I excuse myself to talk to him, leaving Vanni in the large circle of dancers. I watch him for a moment. Soaking him in. He is as comfortable here as in the training yard.

Raised not only at court, but by a king. Of course he is comfortable in this hall. With men like Lord Bailor.

"You've not taken your eyes off him all evening," Kipp comments blandly.

I remind myself this feast is being held to celebrate his return with his men. So instead of quipping back, I search Kipp's eyes for a hint of acceptance. There is none.

"You do not like him."

His answer is immediate.

"Nay. I am surprised you do, given your mistrust of those in power."

"You mean those who might condemn me for my beliefs?"

Even Kipp can recognize Vanni is not such a man.

"Like Father Beald?" I add.

Finally, a hint of a smile.

"I can hardly believe I did that with so many to witness it. I thought of Amma telling me not to give people permission to treat me poorly. And after so many insults . . . I just reacted."

Kipp's brows rise. "Did any seem surprised? If they did, they mustn't know you well, Aedre."

My jaw drops in mock anger. "I've not once slapped a man before."

Kipp chuckles. "'Tis not what I've heard."

"Och, that was *not* a slap. 'Twas a punch. And Agnar deserved it."

Vanni kisses the hand of the white-haired but still somewhat attractive woman he'd been dancing with before coming toward us.

"He is not a man for you, Aedre."

I realize I've been caught staring again.

"Of course he is not. Vanni will be leaving soon."

"Vanni," he mutters. And for the first time I wonder how Kipp will react to learning the king who cast him aside as a babe treated Vanni as a son. I can't imagine it will please him.

"You would like him, I believe. If you give him a chance. He reminds me of you."

The sound Kipp makes is not a pleasant one.

"I am *nothing* like the Curia Commander."

In many ways not. And yet, they share a deep sense of honor and loyalty. Of commitment to the causes they support. Still, it is clear they'll never be friends, at least not tonight, so when Vanni approaches us, I suggest we take our leave.

"There is no need," Kipp interrupts. "I will see Lady Aedre home."

Vanni says nothing but looks to me instead.

"Nay, you will not. This feast is for you, you stubborn goat. I will be well taken care of."

Kipp does not back down. "I am afraid of as much."

"Ugh." I shove away from him and start toward the door. Thankfully, Vanni follows me. I would take my leave from Lord Bailor, but he is currently dancing with his wife. Instead, I find the steward.

"Please give Lord Bailor our thanks for such a wonderful feast."

The steward grins. "And many thanks for the entertainment, Lady Aedre."

I once assisted the steward's wife when she fell ill with standard healing practices, and he has not stopped thanking me ever since. In truth, I'd been terrified as it was the very first time I treated someone without Amma by my side.

"They will be talking about that slap for some time," I comment to Vanni as we walk toward the entrance.

"I should think so."

Something has changed in his tone. Looking up, I see that my companion, who has been so pleasant and cheerful all eve —with the exception of the Father Beald incident, of course —is much more serious now. Nay, not serious but thoughtful.

And I think, as a Garra, I know what that look is about. My core clenches as I consider our ride back to the village, of Vanni's hand clenched around my waist. Of his whispered words in my ear. I know not how this eve will end, but I do know the feast was just the very beginning.

CHAPTER TWENTY-FOUR
VANNI

"*I* would not have you take me home just yet."

If I thought the ride to Anbarth Castle difficult, this ride has been pure hell. I could never have predicted the events of the evening, all of which have made it nearly unbearable to have Aedre so close to me.

With the future so uncertain for my country, my king, I know at least one thing for sure.

I've fallen for this beautiful, feisty healer who has as much courage as the men I lead. I crave her touch. Her gaze. Her words. Every time Aedre looks at me, I want to pull her to me and claim her as my own.

But I have no such claim. Nor will I ever.

And now this, when I've tried so very hard to be respectful. A gentleman.

I know what I should do—say no. Take her back to her father. To her grandmother. To safety. And yet, I find myself saying, "Where would you have us go, if not home?"

"The rocks? 'Tis nearly a full moon."

Indeed, which makes it easy to ride without the benefit of a lantern. But the moonlight, along with the sound of water striking against the cliffs we pass, creates a near magical atmosphere, one which will make it harder yet to stay away from her.

The loveliest faces are to be seen by moonlight, when one sees half with the eye and half with the fancy.

My trainer, Albertus, had many sayings. Matteo and I often asked him where he'd acquired them. In answer to our questions, he would only reply, "From life."

"Vanni?"

Lulled into distant memories of the past, I tighten my arm around Aedre.

"Tell me your thoughts," she says quietly.

She truly is an expert at reading moods. At least my moods.

"I thought of Albertus. And of Matteo."

"You've not said much about him."

Because talking about the Prince of Meria would be akin to admitting he is gone, forever. Which, of course, he is. Along with so many others.

"A highly skilled swordsman, he is . . ."

Was. No longer *is*.

"He was quick to temper at times, but otherwise he was very much like his father. Kind. Loyal. The blood of kings ran through him, and no one could deny it. He would have made a fine leader."

"You must have lost so many people you knew that day."

My fist clenches over the reins.

"I should have been with them, but Galfrid insisted both Ren and I stay behind to prepare for a possible counter-attack. One that is still likely coming."

"Ren?"

The slope gives way to flatter ground as we approach the village.

"He is second commander. Also a member of the Curia."

"And you think Edingham will still attack?"

If only I knew for certain.

"If they do not, certainly Queen Cettina is planning something. We attempted to send over two hundred men to her shores. It matters not that her Borderers gave us just cause."

"I've heard the queen harbors problems of her own."

"You are well-informed."

I make a fateful turn, tugging on Dex's reins just slightly.

"The return of her sister and brother-in-law will not prevent a counter-attack, I don't believe. As much as I wish she were distracted by them. I fear dark days ahead if . . ."

I hate that Aedre is involved in this. But there's no denying her close relationship with Kipp, even though, after this eve, I am reassured it is not a romantic one.

Why should that matter?

It should not. But it does.

"If Kipp does not return with you."

In answer, I guide Dex to a hitching post and dismount. Reaching up, I take Aedre's hand, neither of us commenting further on our destination. Tying off Dex, glad for the post given there are no trees nearby, I pat him on the neck and turn toward the water.

Aedre falls in step with me, and though I itch to give her my hand once more, she navigates the rocks easily without me. Finally, we arrive at our rock. Unable to resist any longer, I take her hand with the intention of helping her to arrange her gown beneath her.

Instead, I pull her toward me, giving in to the temptation that has taunted me from the very moment she walked into the courtyard at the inn this eve. I kiss her with all of the need and longing that has built up inside me, barely waiting for her mouth to open before I plunge inside.

Our tongues tangle, her reactions are anything but timid,

as if she, too, has been waiting for this from the start. I'm the one who pulls away.

"I vowed to protect you. Even from me."

Aedre is not playing this game.

"I don't want protection from you, Vanni."

Pressing myself against her, I try to make her understand.

"You may not want it, but you need it. I will be leaving—"

She presses her finger to my lips.

"I'd know some measure of pleasure from a man I . . ."

My heart skips a beat.

". . . desire," she finishes.

Desire.

It is enough, I suppose.

"I am not so innocent to believe there is just one way for a man and woman to find pleasure."

Of course she isn't. But having no experience with a woman who is both a virgin and a Garra, I've no notion of how to proceed without offending her.

Waves crash along the cliffs in the distance, the water's edge not reaching us this far back.

"This is no bedchamber. And I'm no despoiler of virgins, Aedre."

Especially not you.

"Kiss me, Vanni."

I would do that, and so much more. Kiss her. Be inside her.

Love her.

HE WARS with his sense of honor, but I've no more patience for it. So I pull Vanni's head toward mine. When our lips meet this time, I know they won't part anytime soon. His tongue tangles with mine, and all at once, Vanni's hands are everywhere. As gulls cry above us, the gentle protector becomes something more.

A warrior.

Intent on winning . . . me. But Vanni does not realize his battle is already won. I'm so enjoying every nip and lick of his lips that it's only when the breeze reaches my bare thigh that I realize he's managed to pull up the hem of my skirts.

The very intimate touch should be shocking to me. Instead, I only feel excitement and a rush of warmth between my legs. And then, before I can form a coherent thought, his hand is there.

Cupping me.

When Vanni's groan reverberates through our kiss, I press against him, emboldened by the knowledge that I too am bringing him pleasure. It drives me to kiss him harder, faster.

And then his fingers enter me, slowly at first. His fingers match the rhythm of our kiss perfectly, Vanni every bit as much of an expert at this as he is at combat.

Every thrust is an answer to my years and years of questions. Why are so many afraid of me, my grandmother, my ancestors? Why does Father Beald threaten me so? Why does the very idea of healing hearts and exploring love scare so many?

This is why. We feel more keenly than others, and even for those not so in tune with the healing arts of love surely must understand this as the most incredible feeling in the world.

I whimper against his onslaught, my body clenching in response. Tighter and tighter as his palm rests against me. Presses while his fingers continue to tantalize.

Unable to withstand the intensity any longer, I give over to it. Separated from my body, if only for a moment, I cry out and pull away, even as I press into his hand. Vanni watches me, I realize.

That watching is my undoing.

Exploding into him, I struggle to breathe.

The corners of his mouth tug upward, his sweet smile at odds with what he's so deftly done to me. When he lowers his hand and rearranges my dress, letting it fall to the ground, so many thoughts flit through my mind. Many of which I dare not utter aloud, for I have learned to trust my intuition, and I know no other man can do to me what Vanni has done just now.

"How do you feel?" he asks softly.

As if I can answer such a question simply.

He cups my face in his hands.

"I would give you that, and more, were I able, Aedre."

Why are you not able?

The question lingers on my lips. I do not voice it aloud, however, as I already know the answer. I may have captured a very small piece of Vanni's heart, but the whole of it belongs to the king.

His father's mentor.

The man who raised him.

And who could possibly compete with a king?

Certainly not I.

Still pulsing from his ministrations, his hands now gentle where they were powerful and commanding just a moment ago, I struggle to get out the words.

But I do, nonetheless.

"And I would take it."

CHAPTER TWENTY-FIVE
VANNI

"*G*rab your opponent's arm and strike with your pommel or guard. Be sure to trap their forearm with your second arm, like this."

Agnar is a more patient student than I expected.

As it has been for the past several days, a crowd has gathered to watch our practice. The fishermen have left the inn's courtyard already, off to sea, but enough men remain to give us an audience. But I ignore them as I instruct the Voyager and my squire both.

"Slip the blade against their forearm." Agnar does so to Christopher.

"Use your second hand," a voice booms behind me, "to hold the blade while striking. Or slicing."

Kipp.

A most unexpected guest for our training. Aedre had said he would send for me today, but I hadn't expected him to appear here at the inn, especially not so early . . .

Galfrid's son is full of surprises.

Agnar doesn't hesitate to do just as Kipp suggested, which

tells me all I need to know of Kipp in terms of how the others see him. Voyagers are not quick to follow orders.

"Can you trip or kick your opponent while holding the blade?"

I look at Kipp, who nods. "Aye. You can, and should, do whatever is necessary to win."

"See if you can practice that maneuver with my squire," I suggest.

Agnar grins at Christopher in a way that makes me wonder if leaving the lad with him is ill-advised. He will quickly learn the men of Murwood fight differently than Southerners.

"I'd not expected you here."

Kipp, still leery of me, says nothing. Instead, he walks toward the door of the inn. He pauses before it, looking at me, but at my nod, we head inside.

At this hour, few patrons frequent the hall. By midday, it will be filled with fishermen and those who earn a living along the quay. My men and I are the only visitors, Sailor's Inn more like a tavern most days than a lodging for travelers.

"Two ales?" the innkeeper calls to us. "Welcome home, Master Kipp."

While Kipp greets the man, I lower myself into a chair at the table my men and I have sat at each day for meals. The day is warm, the inn's shutters wide open, giving me a view of the docks.

What Murwood lacks in color—in d'Almerita bright reds and oranges are everywhere even during winter months—it makes up for in fresh sea air and a grit that I can admire. There are fewer luxuries here, but I've never had much need for anything.

Until now.

As Kipp talks to the innkeeper, who pours our drinks, I

think of last eve. Of Aedre. Of her expression when she came apart in my hands. And of her words.

I would take it.

When I said I wished to give her more, I meant it. For the first time in my life, I find myself yearning for something other than a peaceful Meria.

"A meeting," Kipp says, slamming a tankard in the middle of the table. "For Aedre."

The message is clear: if it weren't for her, he wouldn't have accepted this meeting. There's a stubborn edge to this man, and for the first time I let myself acknowledge this might not happen. He might not come.

You must try.

Though the only other people in the hall are the innkeeper, two servants, and two older men sitting clear across the room, I lower my voice, getting straight to the point.

"I know Aedre told you of the shipwreck. Two hundred men perished, including the prince."

"Two hundred men to attack Edingham?"

His tone reeks of disapproval.

"After Saitford was attacked in the middle of the night. A Borderer set fire to the village, claiming nearly half of those who lived there. Women and children included."

When Kipp recoils at that, my hopes are buoyed a bit.

"Could the king not have appealed to Queen Cettina?"

The way he says "the king" leaves no doubt: Kipp hates his father. I cannot blame him for it, but Galfrid wishes to atone for his mistake . . . and the only way he can is if Kipp grants him an audience.

"Their last negotiation left the very man responsible for the attack in charge of the Marches in Edingham."

A buffer on both sides of the river had been agreed to, anger at the Highlanders for having left Meria lingering even so many years later often boiling to a bubble. Or sometimes spilling over the pot.

Kipp makes a sound of disgust. "You mean Death Mountains?"

A term I dislike.

"Calling them so incites the Borderers to the very kind of violence that saw so many innocent people die in Saitford."

"Yet your king's solution to the violence is more violence?"

"He makes decisions with the Curia's input. If you disagree with them, blame me as well as Galfrid."

Kipp shrugs. "Very well. Then you are equally culpable."

"Unlike you, we do not have the luxury to be so separated from our enemy that they can be ignored."

Though not impossible to cross, the Loigh Mountain are a natural barrier between Murwood and both nations. Murwood is easily reached by sea, of course. Yet they remain stubbornly independent from the rest of the Isle.

"We can debate the merits of the attack, but I can assure you, Master Aldwine, the character of the king's nephew is not in question. None who know him think he will be anything but a disaster, both for the Kingdom of Meria and for those who are close to us. The king will never name him as heir."

From Aldwine's expression, it's obvious he knows his cousin's reputation well.

"Lord Hinton will take the throne by force?"

"He will not need to. The church sees his survival as a sign from God of his divine right to rule. In truth, it's naught but a sign of his weakness. Hinton was on the vessel but disembarked before it sailed. They say he had no stomach for it after a night of drinking."

If Aldwine was disgusted before, he is more so now.

"The Prima is a fool, his followers even more so for their

blind allegiance to him. I've no qualms with the church's teachings, but Father Silvester has led too many astray."

I drink, not disagreeing with him. But many in Meria would do so. Unfortunately, some find it difficult to separate the flawed leadership of the church from the religion they practice.

Despite the hard edge of Aldwine's tone, I am more hopeful as he continues to listen and ask questions.

He tilts his head, studying me. "What did Father Beald do to earn your ire?"

An abrupt change of subject, but it is an easy enough question to answer.

"He threatened Aedre and spoke ill of Lady Edrys. In this very hall."

Aldwine grabs his mug, his expression neutral, and sits back against the wall behind his stool.

"You care for Aedre?"

Every word he speaks sits atop a sword's edge. Kipp Aldwine is not a man I would wish as an enemy.

"Aye."

"Yet you will leave here, never to return?"

He stares at me with an intensity that matches—or exceeds—the look Aedre's father gave me, and the inquiry in his eyes reminds me of her grandmother. The question is not a foreign one. I've been asking myself the same thing, over and over, since last eve.

After leaving Aedre, I returned to the very spot where she allowed me to give her pleasure. Where we spoke at length for the first time. Where, against the background of stormy seas, she crept inside my soul.

I imagine riding from Murwood End, looking back to watch her as I take my leave. The image fills me with despair. And yet, I likely won't be able to return. Meria is poised on the brink of war. With itself. And with Edingham, always.

Nor is it an option to bring her with me. I know she will never leave her family.

Another thought haunts the back of my mind. I lose focus here in Murwood. There is a reason the Shadow Warriors take the same vow of celibacy as the men they serve. If I marry, I'll worry more about my wife's safety than my king's.

I take a sip of ale, trying to calm my seething thoughts. "We were discussing the church and Meria's future."

I don't think Aldwine will let it go, so I'm not surprised when he says, "Neither the church nor the future of Meria concerns me overly much."

"And when Lord Hinton becomes king, do you not care for his distaste of the Voyagers' independence from Merian rule? His thirst for war?"

It is the best argument I have, knowing Aldwine cares little about the south and even less for his father.

"If Hinton attempts to take Murwood End, many lives will be forfeit for the effort."

He says it with such calm certainty that I don't doubt him.

By sea, they are unmatched. By land, any advantage of larger numbers will be lost with the difficulty of fighting in the difficult terrain of the Loigh Mountains. The potential gain too little for such a steep price. But Hinton might be dull-witted enough to try it, his distaste for the "savages" well known.

"That'll be little comfort to those who die on both sides. We need you, Aldwine," I state plainly. "Your father needs you."

His only reaction is to take a long swig of ale. Mug empty, he leans forward to fill it from the tankard.

"My father was killed fourteen years ago."

"I'm sorry for that," I say sincerely. "He was, as I understand, quite a man."

For the first time, Aldwine loses his bored, unattached manner.

"You were trained by the Legion of Ash," he says.

I fill my own mug. I'd suspected he would pick up on that. The move I showed Agnar and Christopher was one any with similar training would recognize.

"I was." Though I don't think it will help my cause, I'd be honest with him. "And so was your brother."

He does not react to that.

"My father served Galfrid. When my parents died, your . . . the king raised me at court. I was trained with the prince."

With so few members of the Legion remaining, it is likely Aldwine and I are two of the last men to have been trained by them.

He snorted. "He should name you his successor."

He said it casually, without bitterness or malice. Aldwine does not seem to resent the fact that Galfrid raised me as his own. Worse, he genuinely seems not to care. Kipp Aldwine sees Galfrid as his father as much as I see Father Beald as a man of God, and he is utterly indifferent about our cause.

"He would name his son instead."

Again, no reaction. Thankfully, he seems less inclined to challenge me to a duel than he was on our first meeting. But my words do not seem to have moved him.

"His son, I am sorry to say, is dead."

I look around, ensuring we are not overheard. But none are looking our way or are even within earshot.

"Prince Matteo is dead, aye. But you are very much alive. And if you would return with me to d'Almerita, the king would name you as his successor. And Meria would be better for it. You are clearly a natural leader."

I hold his gaze, Aldwine looking at me with equal parts confidence and challenge. I hold my breath, waiting for his reaction. Though I could continue listing all of the reasons he should come with me, I do not doubt Aldwine already understands the ramifications of his decision. Nor will it help to tell him that the king sent him and his mother here, in the company of a man he handpicked to keep them safe. That Galfrid has routinely sent men here to check on his well-being. But he's been told as much in the past; if it didn't move him then, it won't now.

"Come back with me," I implore him once more.

He opens his mouth to answer me.

CHAPTER TWENTY-SIX
AEDRE

"*A*mma?"

The sun has barely risen, but Father has already gone to the forge. As is my custom, I came into Amma's bedchamber to bid her farewell before taking stock of any herbs I might need, but she's still abed.

"Amma?"

Normally, she wakes easily, but not this morn. She doesn't stir. She doesn't even move. Something is terribly wrong. I run to her bedside, repeating her name, only to realize she's breathing much too heavily. I tear off her coverlet and examine her carefully, finding nothing else amiss except for her legs, which have both swelled. Lowering my head to her chest, I listen carefully.

And dislike what I hear.

Stepping back, I search frantically around the room. Our herbs are not located in here, of course, but it takes me a moment to remember that. To think. To plan. Amma has always praised me for having a calm disposition in uncertain times, but I'm finding it hard to cling to a single thought as I stare down at the only woman I've known as a mother, watching as she struggles to breathe.

Already knowing what this means, wishing I did not, I wipe away the tears in my eyes. It's then I hear her voice in my head. *Long, slow, deep breaths, child. You'll not help anyone like that.*

Finally, I can think.

I need foxglove leaf. And my father.

Running from the room, I make my way to the small healing chamber Father built, despite his hesitations about my calling, and begin to sift through the wooden boxes. I already know we do not have what I need, but I search for it anyway. It's not there, of course.

Deep breaths, Aedre.

I do not wish to leave her, but she needs that plant. Fighting my impulse to return to Amma's chamber, I run out the front door and do not stop. I tear through the field that doesn't grow the plant I need, the soil not sour enough, and make my way toward the village, toward the cottage of the cobbler's wife, where I last saw some. Not willing to veer away from my path, I shout a message to Agnar, who is making his way toward me.

"Tell my father Amma is unwell. I go to Anna for foxglove leaf."

I don't wait for his response. "He is at the forge. Tell him!"

By the time I arrive at the cobbler's home, shouting for Anna, I've found the calm determination that I need to help my grandmother.

"I need foxglove. 'Tis for Amma," I say as Anna emerges, obviously having seen me coming.

"Go," she says. "Go."

I head around to the back, and without stopping to admire the pink blooms, I grab handfuls of leaves, thanking Anna, who wrings her hand on a stained apron. "Is she . . . ?"

My heart knows the answer, but I refuse to say it aloud. Instead, I thank her again and run back, knowing by now the village will have been alerted.

Indeed, by the time I return home, a crowd has gathered outside the house.

I push my way through them, not noticing any faces, intent on my one purpose: to bring Amma comfort.

Whipping open the door, I run inside and head straight to my healing chamber. Getting immediately to work, I grind the leaves into a paste, mindful that the wrong amount will do more harm than good. By the time I finish, adding water to the mixture, and return to her chamber, Father is there, sitting beside her.

"She must drink this," I say, showing him the mug. He does not question me, but rather helps by lifting her head. Some of it dribbles down the sides of her mouth. Some of it she swallows. "That's enough," I say, and Father gently lays Amma's head back onto the pillow.

We exchange a glance, but I can't speak. Neither, it seems, can my father. For all their bickering, he loves and relies on Amma just as much as I do. Holding her hand, he watches as I move to the other side of the bed and do the same. I sit on the edge of the mattress, trying to feel reassured by the slight heat of her against me.

"'Tis her heart," I say.

He asks the silent question, and I shake my head gently.

Amma has been getting weaker for some time. But just the day before she was as spry as ever, it seemed, even making the walk to the forge to sit outside the shop and greet passersby as she so enjoyed doing. And when I came home last eve, she was awake. Waiting for me.

"How was your evening child?" But a smile stole across her face before I could answer her. "Ah, Aedre. Of all the men in the world."

Whether because of her experience as a Garra or her knowledge of me as my amma, she knew. She must have sensed the change in me.

"She seems to breathe easier now," Father says, his tone uncertain.

I will Amma to open her eyes. But she does not.

Looking at Father does not make this any easier. Although he must have shed tears about my mother, I was not old enough to remember them. I cannot recall ever seeing wetness in his eyes. I hope their last words were not said in anger, as the two disagreed on many things.

"She seemed well last eve," I whisper, squeezing her hand but getting no response back.

"Aye," he says, his apron still black with soot. Father always cleans himself, as I do, before coming inside, so it is alarming to see him this way in Amma's bedchamber.

He looks up at me.

"I told her no."

What is he talking about?

"I told Edrys of the invitation, and she begged me to tell you I was too tired to attend. When I realized what she was about, I told her it was completely unacceptable for an unmarried man to escort you, especially one not even from Murwood."

That did sound very much like my father.

"She pleaded with me. And so I relented."

I try to make sense of his words, but I cannot.

"Amma is dying, Father."

He nods as tears well in my eyes, escaping onto my cheeks. When he looks behind me, I do not turn around but feel the bed sink next to me.

Kipp brings my head to his shoulder as the tears fall in earnest. My chest constricts as his arm goes around me. For a few moments, I give myself over to the sorrow, to the tears, and then I lift my head and look down.

Open your eyes, Amma. Give me one last bit of advice. Tell me how to live without you.

But she does not open them. As Father said, she does breathe easier, but it is little consolation. I tell Kipp so he is prepared.

"She is dying," I whisper.

"I know."

I lean forward to kiss my sweet Amma on the cheek, remembering something else she said to me last eve. "Goodnight, child. All will be well."

Why had she not added "in Murwood," as was her custom? And why did I not stay with her longer? Had I known, I would never have left this chamber . . .

A chill runs through me. I know before either Father or Kipp do. I know because the blood of the Garra runs through me. I know, even though I wish I did not.

Lying atop her chest, I wrap my arms around her and weep. Begging her to come back to me. I feel Kipp's hand on my shoulder, and I hear but do not comprehend my father's comforting words, all while I weep and weep and weep.

When I sit up finally, everything hurts. My heart most of all.

Refusing to leave her, even after Father and Kipp do, I sit with Amma for so long day turns into night. I turn both of them away multiple times. How can I leave when the next time I see her it will be on a ship that carries her out to sea, never to return again?

"Aedre?"

Though the sun has already fallen, the chamber is bright courtesy of candles someone, I know not who, has lit. But I would have recognized his voice even if I could not see him.

Vanni.

I jump from the bed, feeling a wave of relief that he has not yet left Murwood. Sometime earlier I had thought of him. Wondered if he and Kipp had spoken after all. But the thought came and went, drowned in the well of sorrow within me.

"You're still here."

He is at my side so quickly, I do not have time to think. Within moments, I'm wrapped in his arms.

"Shhh," he whispers in my ear. But I cannot. My tears refuse to be silent ones. "I am so sorry."

It feels different to be held by Vanni than it did with Kipp. His chest is just as hard and unforgiving, though the pulse of his heart soothes me. Eventually, I stop crying, although I cannot bring myself to move from the safety of his embrace just yet.

"She's gone."

I strain my neck to see his face. But I will not let go of him. Not yet.

"I know she is, Aedre. And I am so sorry for it."

He tries to pull me away with him.

"You must come with me."

And then I realize Father sent him in here to force me to leave Amma's chamber.

"I wish it were otherwise, Aedre, but I know death," he says softly. "Sometimes I feel that I am cursed."

I do break away then, enough to look at him.

"Nay, you are not cursed," I say, sure of my words. "You have seen death, but somehow, though I can't explain it precisely, it is a good thing too."

He looks at me strangely.

"I do not have clear visions as my mother did, but feelings . . ." I shrug. "Aye. Amma says some Garra are given that gift, and by knowing yourself, it can be honed. Maybe someday they will be more clear, but for now, 'tis just a feeling. And with you, there is somehow good to come of the death that surrounds you."

"It is what I meant to say, Aedre. That I know death, and wanting never to rise again because of it. But you will. You must. For the living. For whatever purpose that makes each day worth living."

For a moment, I think he means me, but I know his purpose is the king. And mine? It is what Amma trained me to do.

From the look in his eyes, Vanni thinks I mean to refuse him, but I know I cannot stay here any longer. I must say goodbye.

Moving away and sitting beside her once again, I take Amma's hand and tell her, even though I do not believe the words, "All will be well. I love you, Amma."

If she can somehow hear me, I want her to think her last words to me might hold some truth.

Vanni is there when I stand up again.

"You did not leave," I repeat. Grateful.

"Of course not. I've been outside all day."

I know he has an important mission, one that cannot wait. But I need to know . . .

"Will you stay until the morrow? When we send her off?"

He does not hesitate.

"Aye, Aedre, I will be there, by your side if you wish it."

It's foolish of me to ask. Delaying his departure is not the same as preventing it. Besides, I have Father and Kipp, both of whom have known Amma, and me, my whole life. But knowing that Vanni will be there too, I look back, one last time. And sigh.

I love you, Amma.

I'm ready to leave.

CHAPTER TWENTY-SEVEN
VANNI

"Will you talk to him again?"

Thomas seems uncomfortable with the jubilant atmosphere, a very different kind of ceremony than we're accustomed to in the south. I'll admit, it's my first experience of a Voyager funeral, and I understand—if not share—his unease. We all stood and watched as Aedre's grandmother drifted out to sea on a small boat stacked with her most prized possessions. The moment was strange yet moving, and in its wake the townspeople have gathered for a feast.

It's nothing like the somber ceremonies we're accustomed to in Meria.

I watch as Aedre makes her way through the crowd, smiling as the villagers vie for her attention. I know Aedre's smile is not entirely genuine, but none of the others seem to notice. As she told me earlier, those who come to mourn take their cue from the family, and Lady Edrys wished for her life to be remembered with joy, not pain.

"I'd not planned on doing so. His answer was clear enough."

Following Thomas's gaze, I see Kipp lift a small child off the ground and swing her over his head. His gentleness and his playfulness is so at odds with the man I spoke with at the inn.

"No. I will not return with you," he said. "Not now. Not ever. The man you serve is nothing to me. He is not my father, nor my king. Meria's problems are not mine."

Though I'd expected his refusal by then, his words shook me all the same. I tried again, of course, but my further efforts failed just as surely.

"We cannot go back without him," Thomas says as a serving maid refills both of our mugs. The amount of ale that has flowed since sunset could rival any feast at court. Lady Edrys, beloved by all, is receiving a fine send-off indeed.

"He will not be swayed. We have no choice."

This isn't the first time we've had this conversation. And it will likely not be the last.

Another song starts, this one led by a flute off in the distance, and seemingly every person in attendance begins to sing. Thomas and I exchange a look. The tune is upbeat and joyful, but the words speak of darkness and death. A curious combination.

"We leave on the morrow?" he asks over the singing around us.

I don't answer.

How can I leave Aedre now?

How can I justify staying any longer when Hinton is even now gathering support for his claim? I'm needed in d'Almerita. We all are.

And Galfrid needs to know that Aldwine has rejected his offer. He will have to formulate a new plan, and quickly.

"Aye." Knowing what I must do does not make the decision any easier.

Aedre looks at me. Her smile falters, and I see the deep

pain behind it. The pain she only feels comfortable showing to me, for some reason. She needs me.

"Or perhaps the following day," I say, striding toward her. I can feel Thomas's eyes on my back, but we can make up time on our journey home. It is just one day.

"How do you fare?" I ask as I reach her. She gestures to indicate she can't hear me above the singing, and we move to the edge of the crowd. There are easily over three hundred people here, gathered on the edge of the village, not far from our spot.

"How do you fare?" I ask again when we are separated from the others.

The words feel insufficient. I would prefer to hold her in my arms again, the way I did in her grandmother's chamber. It felt as if she belonged there.

"'Twas a beautiful ceremony, was it not?" she says.

"Aye, it was."

Aedre looks as if she wants to say something, but hesitates.

"Tell me," I prompt her.

As the singing dies down, the soft lapping of the waves is once again evident. We're far enough away that none seem to notice us here, and we stand side by side, watching the revelry from afar.

"When I came home the night of the feast, she told me all would be well."

The need to hold her nearly overwhelms me this time, but with her protectors close by, I dare not.

You are her protector too.

I shove away the thought.

"I said nothing to her . . . nothing about us, I mean. I was too embarrassed. But she knew something had happened anyway."

I can't help but smile. "A Garra, embarrassed?"

But Aedre doesn't smile with me. Of course she doesn't. Her Amma just passed away.

She looks down at her feet. "I do not deserve that title."

"Of course you do." Lifting Aedre's chin, I force her eyes to mine. "Of course you do," I repeat. "Why would you say such a thing?"

Now that I'm touching her, I don't want to break our contact, however small.

"I never truly understood desire . . . love."

Until now, no feeling has ever matched my yearning for my parents to be alive again. My drive to please the king. My devotion to my country. But this longing I feel for Aedre is so deep it stays with me, waking or asleep, and resurfaces at all hours. Every muscle in my body aches to hold her. To comfort her. Every thought in my head is for or of her.

But your situation hasn't changed, a voice in my head reminds me.

Reluctantly, I drop my hand.

"Can a motherless woman care for a child?" I say.

"Aye, for certain."

"Can a midwife help a woman give birth to a new babe even if she's never carried?"

Understanding glimmers in her eyes, and she nods. "You will leave on the morrow."

She changed the topic utterly without warning, but I'm becoming accustomed to her ways. To her habit of cutting to the point.

"Nay," I decide, knowing the men will not agree. They have reason to object, and yet . . .

Had Aldwine not returned, we'd still be waiting for him.

"I would meet you," I say.

If but for one last time.

Aedre glances at the crowd before she answers, and part

of me fears she'll say no. Mayhap she should. "I would like that very much."

"Come, we'll find your father."

Though I want to take her hand as we walk back, I have no right to do so.

"I'm sorry, Vanni," she says quietly. "I know Kipp has told you he'll not go south."

It moves me so much that she's thinking of my disappointment, after losing such an important person in her life, and I find it hard to answer. Instead, I stop and look into her eyes.

She seems to understand.

I am sorry too. About Kipp. About Lady Edrys.

About us.

ll day I've waited for him, working alongside my father, letting the hammer's rhythmic strike on the anvil lull me into some sort of peace. Not the kind that stays with you, but the fleeting kind that keeps the demons at bay.

But it never lasts for long. No more than a few minutes pass before I'm reminded that Amma isn't sitting just outside the forge. Or the door will open, and I'll look up, expecting Vanni to fill the frame. Instead, it'll be a patron of my father's or his apprentice, Amery.

This time, it's neither.

"Agnar," I greet him from my perch on a high stool. Punching is my least favorite duty, but it needs to be done. Still, if there's any excuse to stop, I'll take it.

"A ship has just arrived," he announces.

"A regular occurrence here, but thank you for the information, Agnar," Father says. He has not lost his humor, at least.

"From Breywood."

Not a regular occurrence. We trade regularly with Highlanders, but almost never with the Edingham royal court. It is most unusual indeed.

"Breywood Castle?" I clarify.

"Aye," Agnar says. "They say the queen's commander is on the ship." He scowls. "We've one too many of those already in Murwood."

That surprises me.

"I thought you and Va . . . Lord d'Abella have gotten on? From what I hear, you've been training with him."

In answer, he grumbles something and nods toward the door. "Are you coming?"

When an interesting ship comes to port, many of the villagers gather to meet it. I shake my head, about to say no, when Father answers for me.

"Take her. Go, Aedre."

Normally my father is attempting to get me into the forge, not out of it. I'm about to ask the reason for the sudden change when I realize he's attempting to distract me.

Mayhap I need to be distracted.

"Go," he says, more forcefully than is his custom. "Bring back news of the visitors."

"I will finish that," Amery says, taking the punch from me and gently guiding me off the stool. When I'm next to him, I realize the boy we've come to depend on so much is now a young man.

"When did you grow so tall, Amery?"

He straightens even more. "Some time ago, Lady Aedre."

I smile at him, forgetting for the moment that my world has been turned around, and hand over my tools. Taking off my apron, I hang it and bid Father farewell. I wash outside in the wooden bucket, then join an impatient Agnar, who talks the entire way.

I have little to say.

Amma is gone. Vanni will be leaving. I chastise myself for

not having spoken to him again last eve before I returned home, unable to abide the crowd of revelers any longer.

By the time we arrive, we're not the only ones hoping to get a look at the newcomers.

"I see nothing," I say, angling for a better view.

It's then I realize we've been separated in the crowd. Agnar is nowhere to be seen, leaving me to navigate toward the docks myself. I make my way toward the water's edge and get a glimpse of blue and silver.

Agnar was right. It seems these men are from the queen's court. How peculiar for there to be two commanders in Murwood End at the same time. Does Vanni know about it?

"Oh!" Grabbed from behind, I'm unable to reach my knife in time. But it seems I don't need it.

Vanni pulls me by the hand, guiding me away from the crowd.

"What are you . . ."

Shoved sideways by the press of people, I'm grateful for the anchor of Vanni's hand. He has a tight grip on me and doesn't seem inclined to let go.

"Where are we going?"

"To the inn."

The inn?

Indeed, although it catches me by surprise when he leads me not to the front but through the courtyard—his makeshift training yard—and then up a set of wooden stairs after looking around, presumably to be sure no one is watching.

Vanni released my hand as we first started to climb up, and has yet to say a word to me since.

How did he even see me in that crowd?

Where are we going?

When he opens a door and steps inside, I follow. I'd seen

this back entrance to the rooms on the second floor before, but I've never been up here.

Squeezing past me, Vanni takes out a key and opens the last door at the end of the hallway. He pushes it open, and I follow him in.

"This isn't how I'd planned to meet you today," he says. "I went to the forge this morning." He closes the door behind me. "But you weren't there yet. I'd have returned sooner, but a ship appeared on the horizon and . . ."

He opens the shutters just slightly for air, both sets of them, partially illuminating a small but well-appointed room. There is not much inside but a bed, two chairs, and a wooden stand with a bowl of water and a strip of linen cloth next to it.

"This is where you've been staying."

"Aye."

Before I can ask another question, he's there in front of me.

He takes me in his arms and draws me to him, his lips lowering to mine. I care not that it is highly improper for us to be here, in this room, alone. He is leaving and, like Amma, he will be gone forever. And maybe that's why he dragged me from the docks to be here.

I give him back all of me.

Our tongues tangle in a kiss that consumes us both. A desperate one, at least on my part, born of loss and need to get even closer to him. Something takes over, and that some-thing has me tugging on his tunic, wanting . . . more. Needing it.

Vanni says nothing as he pulls his tunic over his head. He watches me as I stare at his bare chest, now on full display. And when I reach out, hesitant, he covers my hands with his own and presses down, wordlessly giving me permission to explore. My touch is hesitant at first, but then my hands stray everywhere, savoring the warm, hard ridges of his chest. Vanni's groan is the only sound between us, the room as still and silent as the courtyard below.

Everyone but us is down at the docks.

Two brass brooches at my shoulders hold the material of my mantle together. He must know this, because he reaches for them and looses them in but a moment. The overcoat spills to the ground, leaving just a long-sleeved shift behind.

When Vanni pulls me back to him, this time it is an entirely different experience. Without so many layers between us, I can feel his desire for me in every touch. In the melding of our lips. And in the way his hands work their way up from my hips, trailing along my waist and then moving higher. He cups my breasts, both of us all hands and touches, as if desperate to memorize each other. When he kisses my neck and then dips lower, I can no longer remain silent.

"I need all of you."

"Aedre . . ."

"Do not deny me this."

His breath is shallow, as if he were in pain.

"You don't know—"

I press my finger into his chest. "If you tell me I don't know what I'm asking, then I will remind you of who I am. I'm a Garra, Vanni. Like my grandmother before me. I've lost her, but I will *not* lose the chance to be with you before you leave. Maybe we did not plan for this, but you will give me all of you this day."

I can tell he wasn't expecting those words.

Well, I was not really expecting them either. But I will not take them back. If I cannot give my virginity to the man I love, for there is no longer any doubt about my feelings for him, then who should I give it to?

"I did not intend this. I just . . ." Vanni runs a hand through his hair. "I saw you and needed to be with you."

171

I raise my chin. "And you will be. Do not make the same mistake as you did the day we met."

He might have southern sensibilities still, but he should know I am no gentlewoman of his courts. In Murwood End, we can be captains. We can be blacksmiths. We can wield our sexuality as well as any man. We can make decisions for ourselves.

Though he might be relenting, I can see he's still worried.

"I will not grow with child."

I was correct. From the look on his face, that was precisely the source of his concern.

"I know the mysteries of a woman's body. 'Tis not my time to beget a child."

Vanni just looks at me for a moment, regarding me with a look that sends my heart racing. Does he respect me enough to take what I offer?

CHAPTER TWENTY-NINE
VANNI

I didn't mean for this to happen.

I'd thought to speak with her, to kiss her again, and then to leave.

But when I saw Aedre in that crowd, something inside of me would not be held back. Last eve, being so close to her, unable to comfort her as I would have liked . . .

If the rumors are indeed true, I should be down at those docks. I should be trying to determine what Queen Cettina is planning—and how I can stop it. Instead, I'm here, actually contemplating taking this woman's virginity.

I cannot do it.

"Aedre."

My voice sounds foreign to my own ears.

Do not make the same mistake as you did the day we met.

I remember her words that day.

You've much to learn, Southerner.

And I *have* learned much since arriving in Murwood End. I've learned that its people are more than willful and wild. That they're resourceful and intelligent too, Aedre more so than most.

Do not deny me this.

I'm losing the war with myself, my resolve slipping away as she waits for me to decide. This goes against everything I've been taught. If we do this . . .

Never in my days have I disrobed so quickly. As I do, Aedre's keen eyes roam down from my chest, which she'd been admiring, to the evidence of my desire for her. I reach for the hem of her shift and lift it up, Aedre's arms reaching high to assist me.

She kicks off her leather shoes and, seeing her nude, I know my biggest challenge will be to take this slow. As we come together, our bodies blessedly touching everywhere, I wonder if such a thing is even possible. My hands are everywhere, and hers . . . ah God. She cups my backside and my hips jerk forward in response.

Kissing Aedre has become like life to me, as necessary as eating or drinking. And then she does something so unexpected, I hardly have time to react.

"Aedre? What are you doing?"

Kneeling, she wraps her hand around me, as if positioning us both.

"'Tis evident, is it not? You gave me pleasure and I will return it."

She cannot think to . . .

When her lips wrap around me, I clench my fists in her hair, careful to do so gently. At least, I try to be gentle, but this innocent woman takes me in her mouth as skillfully as a practiced courtesan.

Garra, I remind myself. Not experience but having been trained in the art of loving. But it is so unexpected for a woman whose kiss was tentative at first that I know this cannot last. If she continues, I'll spill my seed in her mouth, and I cannot allow that to happen.

Lifting her up is the single hardest thing I've ever done in my life. Her lips are wet, eyes curious. It takes just seconds for me to move us to the bed.

Is this a dream? Will I wake to find this simple chamber empty, Aedre no longer with me? But it feels so very real. Squirming under me, getting into a comfortable position, Aedre stares up at me, her eyes never leaving mine.

As my hands move from her breasts downward in a sweet exploration, I push her thighs open and slip my finger inside to be sure. Aye, she is ready.

But am I?

"You are the most beautiful woman in the Isle, Aedre," I say, hoping she believes that truth. I withdraw and position myself above her, unable to believe this is truly happening.

"This cannot be undone," I say with a groan. "Do not look at me like that, Aedre. I'm determined to take this slowly."

Her hands rest on my shoulders.

"I am no delicate vase, Vanni. I will not break if you drop me."

Positioning myself with my hand, I vow to her, "I will never drop you."

Though I've never taken a woman's virginity before, I know it will cause her pain. Entering slowly, I reach the barrier and wait.

Throbbing. My hands shaking as they hold my body over her.

It feels as if this is my first time making love to a woman, though it's hardly that.

"Aedre?"

I remember the first time she gave me her name. *Aedre, daughter of Dal Lorenson, descendant of Athea.*

And know her answer even before she nods. We will be joined this day.

When she nods slightly, giving me permission, I don't hesitate, wanting the pain to go quickly for her.

She does cry out then, and I'm sorry for it. I still myself, closing my eyes and calming my racing heart . . . or trying to.

Finally, I open them again, hoping her pain has eased.

Aedre looks down between us, curious.

"Does it hurt?"

She blinks, then shakes her head. Smiles.

I start moving then, my hand gliding up to her breast. I would tell Aedre she has captured my heart, but she must know I'd not be inside her if she hadn't. The strain of holding back, of resisting the urge to thrust, makes my arms shake.

Rewarded with a soft whimper, I grow bolder. Move faster. Circle my hips, intent on just one thing.

Giving Aedre more pleasure than she's ever received in her lifetime. I know a part of her has been left vulnerable these past days, her world changing irrevocably. For these brief moments, I want to take away her pain and replace it with the very opposite.

When her hips press upward, I know she's fully recovered. With the first thrust, her eyes widen. With the second, her nails press into the flesh of my arms.

With the third and fourth, she screams out my name, and I welcome it.

"Vanni," she says, over and over again.

Rubbing her nipple between my thumb and forefinger, I angle my body slightly and move again.

"Aedre," I murmur in response, knowing exactly how she feels. I could let go at any moment as she climbs toward that final rush of pleasure.

And then she looks into my eyes.

All of it is there.

Her inital resistance toward me.

The teasing Garra who agreed to "treat" me.

The gentle healer, sorrowful granddaughter, fierce fighter.

Looking down at her, I could no sooner hold back than if she'd continued to take me in her mouth. Thankfully, her face transforms to pure joy as I tumble into my release. I collapse on top of her, holding myself up just enough not to crush her. When her arms wrap around me, I don't even consider moving.

The ship that so distracted everyone will have been abandoned. The villagers will return, the inn filling up below us, making it more difficult to sneak her out. But I just don't care.

My failed mission.

Rumors about the queen's commander.

The king's need for us.

None of it matters more than the woman I just made love to, who is holding me as if she would never let go.

And now we won't have to part. Our joining solves the problem of me having to leave her, though it creates many others.

I lift my head finally, confirming it with Aedre.

"You will come with me to d'Almerita."

Her lips part, and I can feel myself stir again, still inside her.

"Come with you?" She seems genuinely confused.

"Aye. We will marry. And you will come with me."

I don't like the look she gives me.

"You think . . . I want to leave Murwood End because I gave you my virginity? That I'd abandon my father, my whole life?"

I definitely did not expect her anger.

"You think," I counter, "that I would take it today and leave you tomorrow? I never expected this, us, but we have no choice now, Aedre."

What manner of man does she think I am? I've taken her outside of marriage, but to do so and then simply leave her?

"You did not expect me at all? You knew nothing of me and Kipp when you first came here?"

I'm unsure what made her think of that now, but when asked that way, I would not lie to her.

"I knew there was a woman. And I thought perhaps . . ."

Her eyes narrow, fire blazing from them.

"You *knew*."

"Aedre, I did not. It was a possibility, of course, but had little to do with why we met so often. Surely you know that. As you know you are a lady. An unmarried lady, and I've just taken your virginity."

"So Kipp was right. And you did not *take* my virginity, Vanni. I *gave* it to you. There is a difference."

Perhaps, but there is no difference in the outcome.

"You will marry me, Aedre. I am not leaving here without you."

I don't much care for the look she gives me as her hands push against my chest.

"Then it seems as if Murwood End has gained a new resident, because I am not leaving."

CHAPTER THIRTY

VANNI

"There's been a . . . complication," I admit to Thomas as we sit at a table in the inn.

Aedre ran off before I could stop her—her reaction a clear sign that I did not express myself well. Although I still very much plan to press my suit, it's clear she needs time to process everything. To cool down. So I watched her walk away—an experience I didn't care for—and then headed into the great hall of the inn for an ale. Thomas found me there and joined me.

From the look on his face, he's not surprised by my words.

"Aye, I suspected so," he replies. "You left us at the docks."

With good reason, but I don't offer an explanation. "Was it truly someone from the Royal Court of Edingham?"

The serving girl brings Thomas an ale, and he thanks her. I drink from my mug, missing wine more than I would have expected. The bitter ale of the north is a poor substitute, though passable, I suppose.

"If you'd stayed long enough, you might have seen your old friend Stokerton."

"You saw him with your own eyes?" I ask in disbelief. I'd heard the rumor but had not believed it true.

Thomas raises his mug to me. "I saw the queen's second with my own eyes."

In that case, I don't doubt him. The man is difficult to miss. There's always a trail of women following him, hoping for a glimpse or even a wink.

I've met Erik Stokerton on numerous occasions and have come away with two incontrovertible truths:

He is as deadly as he is good-looking.

He is madly in love with his queen.

All know it, and he does not aim to hide the fact. It was rumored she once carried his babe, but naught came of that particular rumor. Though there are others . . .

"What is he doing here in Murwood?"

For a brief moment, fear blinds my thinking. Could he know about Aldwine somehow? Is he here to persuade him to their cause?

Impossible. If Edingham knew of Aldwine, they'd have exploited him long ago.

"We need to speak to him," I say.

Thomas smiles. "Done. He will be joining us tomorrow midday, in this very spot."

We are enemies, aye. But neither side wishes for a full-out war. The queen's Curia would not dare to attack us without provocation. And I plan to give them none.

"How many travel with him?"

He lifts his eyebrows. "If you'd stayed longer, perhaps you would already know."

I know without asking that he saw me leave with Aedre.

"Thomas—"

"Explain to another. I more than anyone understand what it is to love a woman. You'll draw no judgment from me."

He thinks I'm in love with Aedre.

Am I not?

Although I didn't intend to take things so far, part of me is glad for it. I didn't want to be parted from her, and now I won't have to be. Because whatever she thinks, we *will* marry. I will not leave Murwood End without her.

"Tomorrow midday?" The timing of our meeting just occurs to me.

"Aye. He suggested it himself. I also learned he is to be a guest of Lord Bailor." Thomas shrugs. "I suppose that's where the queen's men can be found this eve."

He drinks, unconcerned.

Lord Bailor did not make such an offer to *us* when we arrived. I watch my friend, wondering how he could be so oblivious.

"A guest of Lord Bailor?"

"Aye."

"Why didn't he offer us the same courtesy?"

"Maybe he would have if you were as good-looking as Stokerton."

Laughing at his own joke, Thomas does not seem bothered by my concern. So I lean forward, lower my voice, and enlighten him. "The queen's commander is here, in Murwood End, as a guest of the highest-ranking noble in town. Weeks after our failed attack."

He blinks.

God save me from him.

"And now I know why Galfrid thought so long and hard about naming you Knight Commander," I quip.

Thomas isn't bothered by my words. He's openly admitted he can be quite difficult at times. If he weren't such a fierce warrior . . .

"He is here to gather support."

Thomas stares at me a moment and then laughs. "From the Voyagers? They will not give it. They've always withheld aid and allegiance from both sides."

True, but these are curious times.

"Maybe so, yet it hasn't stopped them from trying in the past."

When Galfrid's father reigned, the War of Loigh claimed more lives than any of the other wars in Meria's history. In a bid to end the fighting, the King of Edingham had sent a contingent of men to Murwood to elicit the aid of the Voyagers. They refused, and none have attempted to solicit their support since.

Some say the Voyagers trade more regularly with Meria because of that long-ago breach of their unwritten rules: Voyagers do not care for any to test their neutrality. Now that I've spent time here, I have a better understanding of their ways. Of their independence. The people here honor Aldwine for his fearlessness more than they do Bailor for his title. Such things are meaningless in Murwood, and the queen should know that already.

But she's accustomed to wealth and power mattering, and here they do not.

"If they *do* get the Voyagers' support . . . ," Thomas begins, but I stop him.

"You are correct—they would never agree to such a thing. But I can tell you, unequivocally, that is why Stokerton is here."

"Hmm. Then it should be an interesting meeting. So, since I went to the trouble of arranging it, perhaps you can tell me more of the complications you have embroiled your-self in."

I have a feeling he already knows. But Stokerton's arrival gives me an unexpected stay of execution. An extra day to speak to Aedre, to make her understand. She thinks my interest in her was solely to gain an audience with Kipp, and I have to convince her otherwise. I was drawn to her from the start, and there is no way I will leave Murwood End without her. Now I have a reason to stay, to convince her that we should marry.

CHAPTER THIRTY-ONE
AEDRE

"*J* will *never* marry him. He knew, Kipp."

Kipp grins at me as I pace in his solar. I came to Nord Manor after sending word to Father instead of going home, desperate to avoid Vanni. I've stayed overnight here before, the manor more than large enough to accommodate guests. Now that the tide has risen, we are accessible only by boat, and Vanni and his men have none. Of course, as Kipp pointed out, they could obtain one easily for the short journey, but I do not believe Vanni will do so.

He was less angry than I imagined when I told him Vanni suspected I knew him. Or at least considered the possibility Kipp and I were friends. If he had any inkling of it, Vanni should have told me when I asked.

Is he even still here, in Murwood End?

This morn, the thought of him leaving was devastating. But now, the very opposite is true. If he had asked me instead of telling me . . . if he had made some profession of love . . . if he had considered my wants and needs at all . . . if he'd mentioned the possibility that he knew I had a connection to Kipp.

I don't know what would have happened then. But I'll not let a man dictate my future out of some allegiance to a code of honor I do not share. Nor will I wed a man who's made it quite clear he has no wish to marry.

I would rather remain here, in the manor house, heartbroken.

"The choice is yours."

Stopping at the window, I find myself thinking of Vanni's chest beneath my hands, of him thrusting into me, of him looking into my eyes with something stronger than lust. Of the utter bliss I experienced with him.

I was ignorant before, but now . . . now I *know*. And I will never, ever be the same again.

"How could you not have told me?" I accuse, knowing my anger is misplaced but unable to help myself.

"Told you what, precisely?"

Unlike me, Kipp is relaxed, legs stretched out in front of him as he eats an apple and fingers the dagger my father forged for him. I'll never forget the day he asked my father for that weapon. Father and I were in the shop when Kipp stormed inside. Normally, we would have learned of his ship's arrival before we saw him, but we'd heard nothing. We only knew he and his father had gone off to fight for Lord Rawlins in Edingham.

But I knew straightaway something had gone wrong. Which was confirmed by Kipp's words.

"I need a dagger. The finest, sharpest one you've ever forged."

Even now a chill runs up my back at the memory of his expression that day.

After explaining that his father had been killed, he stated his intention to slay the man who'd hired him.

Lord Rawlins had gained back his estate but at a great loss of life, something the Highlander cared little about given the majority of the men were hired mercenaries. Worse, he refused to pay Kipp, saying his agreement was with the father, not the son.

Since that day, he's never again spoken of the battle, or of Rawlins, except but one time. I'd asked Kipp why he had wanted a dagger when he owned a perfectly good sword.

"I will look into the eyes of the man responsible for my father's death."

After that, I never asked again about Lord Rawlins, his plans for revenge, or details of the battle. I know only he's talked many times of an opportunity for a fair fight with the man.

"Aedre? What did I not tell you?"

I tear my gaze away from the dagger.

"You've been with women before. How could you not have told me what it was like? How *transformative* it is."

Kipp wasn't exactly happy to learn what happened between Vanni and me, especially since it was as much my idea as Vanni's, but I'm annoyed too. I can't help but feel my friend has been withholding.

"You allowed me to practice what Amma taught me, but I didn't truly understand what I was doing," I continue. "I am a fool."

He does not seem overly concerned.

"What would you have me say, Aedre? 'Tis not something easily put into words. As well you know."

Could I put what I experienced earlier that day into words? The feeling of Vanni inside of me? The bond that had formed between us, so strong I would have thought it unbreakable if he had not snapped it so quickly afterward?

"I am a fool," I repeat, shoving aside the comforting words Vanni spoke the other night. He compared my practice to that of a childless midwife. But it is different. So different.

"Amma knew," Kipp says, his words barely a whisper. "She did not think you less of a Garra because of it."

Amma. I dishonor her memory by worrying about Vanni when I should be mourning.

"What would she say if you told her what you told me about Vanni?"

I only need to consider it for a moment. The answer is as clear to me as my memory of her smile, for she always asked the same thing of the people who came to her for help in matters of love.

"She would have asked if I love him."

Amma had claimed the heart always, always knew, even when the mind did not. And that love was a greater healer than marigold or mallow. No herb or stone or talisman could properly substitute for it. She had loved my grandfather, whom I never knew. And taught her daughter to marry for love too.

"Do you believe in marrying for love, Kipp?"

It's been some time since we've discussed the subject, though I'm sure I already know his answer.

"Few in this world can afford the luxury."

Voyagers might be freer than most, certainly more so than those from Meria or Edingham, but there are disadvantages to living in such a small place.

"Do you suppose I've fallen for Vanni simply because he is *not* from Murwood?" I ask.

Kipp puts the knife down on a table next to him in favor of a mug of ale.

"Fallen? I'd think you of all people would be brave enough to say the word, Aedre."

I slink into a velvet-lined chair across from my friend, the sky now completely dark.

"Love."

Amma always described love as both wondrous and

treacherous, a healer and the source of sorrow. I thought I understood. I love *her*. And Father. And Kipp.

But this is different. This type of love has fangs.

One of Kipp's brows lifts. "Have you *fallen* for any of the other men who've come through here?" he asks. "There are plenty of them, are there not?"

Indeed.

"You have no other words of wisdom?"

Kipp shrugs. "You've made it clear you'll not marry him. What wisdom could I offer? He will leave, if he's not done so already, and you will likely never see the man again."

"You are no Amma," I mutter.

"Nay, I am not."

"Do you truly believe he only cared for me as a way to gain access to you?"

I know better than to think it, but I am curious whether Kipp still believes it to be so.

He gives me a long look and, as if what he saw made him pity me, proceeds to stand and pour me a mug of ale. Once it passes from his hand to mine, he sits again.

"Nay, I do not. I saw the fire in his eyes when Father Beald walked into Lord Bailor's hall. His reaction was not feigned."

Which reminds me. "Speaking of Lord Bailor . . . they say the queen's commander is his guest. Does that not surprise you?"

"Nay, it does not. I expect he will attempt to garner support for an attack on Meria."

I nearly spill the ale halfway to my lips.

"Attack on Meria?"

I hadn't considered why they were here, precisely. Given what happened with Amma. And Vanni. I haven't thought of much else.

"You know as well as I do they are weakened by the loss

of that ship. With a contingent of Voyagers, they could cause real damage. The conflict could finally be resolved."

His words make no sense.

"Voyagers do *not* serve the queen."

"Perhaps for the right price . . ."

Nay, it is not possible.

"You would never."

Kipp gave up his mercenary days when his father died. Although some of his journeys are still dangerous, his focus is on trade, not fighting. Does he hate the king so much he'd consider taking up arms against him? Against Vanni?

"Kipp?"

He makes a face that I do not like.

I'm consumed by the thought of him sailing to d'Almerita, engaging in battle with Vanni. What if Kipp kills him? What if Vanni kills Kipp?

"Kipp?" I ask again, this time more urgently. "We do not involve ourselves in Merian affairs. You cannot. No matter what the price. Please tell me you will not think of it."

When he smiles, that sly, intelligent smile that's so very Kipp, I realize I've been played.

"Have you fallen in love with Lord d'Abella because he's an outsider? I don't believe so, though I can't say I understand what you see in him. Still, you are in love with him, that much is clear. Marry him. Or do not. 'Tis your choice."

He can be such an arse sometimes. But for all his protests, I can tell something has shifted in him, though I don't know when or why. If his dislike for Vanni were as strong as he claims, he wouldn't encourage me to remember one of Amma's greatest lessons.

That we all choose our own fate.

She held that belief more dear, even, than her faith in love.

If only Vanni agreed.

"I do love him," I admit. "I'm not sure how it happened, Kipp. But I do."

Kipp grunts in answer.

"But he just *assumed* I would marry him. That I would leave Murwood End, not to mention Father and you, and join him in d'Almerita. Does he not consider a Garra may not be welcome there? Or that I might not care to swear my allegiance to his king?"

Heated now, my hands flailing, I stop, struck by the knowledge that the king is Kipp's father. That *he* could be the king one day, if he accepted the man's offer.

"Have you thought of it, even for a moment? That you could be the next King of Meria?"

"No."

He's such a liar.

"Not even for one moment? As you lay your head down at night, dreaming of all that is possible? You've not considered it once?"

Kipp's amusement is evident. "Dreaming of all that is possible? Is that what you do?"

I roll my eyes. "So what do *you* think of as you fall asleep?"

He gives me an impish grin that immediately conjures thoughts of Vanni. Of the way he felt on top of me, moving inside of me . . .

"Incorrigible," I murmur.

"While we were in Midenear, there was a widow named—"

"Save your thoughts for the pillow."

Kipp's laugh lifts my spirits as it always does, and reassures me I'm making the right decision. I could never leave him. Or Father. Certainly not for a man who presumes to make decisions for me despite having only known me for a sennight.

Even so, the thought he may have already left Murwood .
. .

What will happen to him if the Voyagers pledge their support and Edingham attacks? Kipp will not participate, I know, but he does not control the others. And what if the king's nephew gains enough support to successfully challenge the king's successor, whomever he chooses? What will happen to Vanni then?

"Aedre?"

I push aside thoughts of a problem I cannot solve.

"We will both remain in Murwood End," I say flatly. If part of me questions it, there's nothing for it. There is no other decision to make.

Kipp raises his mug. "Let us drink in memory of Amma. No talk of Meria or your commander or the king. Aye?"

I lift my mug too, though it feels heavy. "Aye."

With naught left to say, we drink in silence.

CHAPTER THIRTY-TWO
VANNI

*T*his meeting with the queen's commander is reminiscent of the one I had with Aldwine. Same inn, same table. Stokerton gives off the same air of confidence, even, and is approximately the same age.

But the similarities stop there.

Whereas Aldwine is reticent and suspicious by nature, Stokerton is anything but. Every time we've come in contact before, I've been left with the impression that, were we not enemies, the commander and I could be friends.

Good-natured, often smiling or jesting, he is well-liked by most, including the queen. The rumors of Queen Cettina and Lord Stokerton rival even the most scandalous stories about the Merian court. Some say they'd be married already if she were not a queen.

Thomas and I stand to greet the commander and one of his men.

My mind should be firmly on this meeting and what I hope to gain from it, and yet I find my thoughts straying to Aedre. I deliberately did not seek her out last eve, knowing she was wroth with me. But I went to her house this morning, expecting to find her, only for her father to tell me she'd spent the night at Nord Manor.

It was as if her father had punched me in the gut. An unmarried woman, staying overnight as a guest of an unmarried man?

As Aedre herself would tell me, the rules are different here, or rather there aren't any. And I've observed myself that she and Kipp act like brother and sister. Which might comfort me more if the two were related in any way.

A jab in the arm from Thomas pulls me back to the present.

"Lord d'Abella. Sir Thomas. What a fine meeting place you've chosen," Stokerton says. He nods to his companion. "Sir Alex McGreghere."

I shake the older man's hand. As is typical for a Highlander, his grey hair is worn long and loose. But I know better than to discount him because of his age—behind his bushy beard are intelligent green eyes, striking in their color.

"We met once before," the knight says, "many years ago at Castle d'Almerita. I believe it was the very year Galfrid welcomed you there. There was quite a bit of talk about the young boy whose sword skill would someday be unmatched."

Despite myself, I like the man already. He deftly avoided saying *the year your parents died*, and though it amounts to much the same, I appreciate his tact.

"I am sorry to have forgotten it, McGreghere."

We sit then, the two men across from us, a tankard of ale and four mugs already gracing the table.

"You were a boy. And this"—he pulls on his beard—"was more brown than grey then."

"And this," I say as Thomas pours ale into our mugs, "is Sir Thomas Hawthorne."

"The best amongst us," Stokerton says, "for he pours the ale."

My attention shifts to the commander.

As in Meria, the members of the queen's Curia retain their titles for life unless otherwise decreed by the monarch. Which means he will remain as the second commander until the first commander dies. The duties are similar, as evidenced by the fact that we are both here, in Murwood, to do our liege's bidding.

The purpose of this meeting is for me to learn what, exactly, their liege has bid them to do.

"We were surprised to learn of your presence," Stokerton says, getting straight to the heart of the matter.

"As were we," I admit. "You first?"

His laugh makes it impossible not to smile.

"D'Abella is not one for niceties," he explains to McGreghere. "But the rumors are true. He is quite deadly with a sword."

Since there is no hint of malice, I thank him for the compliment. "Unfortunately, it seems I will be forced to use it before I would wish."

Stokerton does not flinch.

"Perhaps if you'd not sent a ship full of your best men against us, such things could have been avoided."

He says it as if reporting that day's weather.

"Word reached the capital quickly. As usual, Breywood is well informed."

"Not as quickly as it reached *you*, it appears. They say you've been in Murwood for near a fortnight now."

Less, but I do not correct him. Nor do I correct his assumption that we've come here to solicit the Voyagers' help. It serves my purpose to let them think such a thing. Clearly, they know nothing of Aldwine, and I would keep it that way. Although he might not join our cause today, or tomorrow, as long as the king's son lives, there is hope he might yet be persuaded. Though not, it seems, by me.

"We were provoked, Stokerton, as well you know."

Thomas adds, "Women and children were never fair game in this fight between us."

To his credit, the commander seems genuinely saddened by the thought. His smile flees.

"That the borders grow more lawless each day should not surprise you. When Galfrid last requested a parley on that very matter, your queen denied him," I say.

At the words "your queen," Stokerton's eyes narrow. "Cettina wants peace along the borders as much as he does."

I try not to laugh, knowing it will only incite him.

"Willing it so will do little to make it happen."

McGreghere jumps in. "I live where the Loigh Mountains meet the Northern Mountains. None wish for peace there more than I do."

A true Highlander, then, living in a place known for its danger.

"Galfrid has forgotten us," he says, which is where I cannot help but jump in.

"He is not your king. Your ancestors saw to that."

And round and round we go, as always, for the rift is bitter and old and full of blame.

Halfway into a second round of ale, I put a stop to the never-ending discussion. "We will not negotiate peace here at this inn, a place where neither of us hold sway." I pause, calculating, then say, "You've also come to solicit the Voyagers' support?"

No matter what Stokerton says, his eyes share the truth of my words. A fool's errand. They will never fight for Edingham.

Or Meria.

"Lord Bailor remained coy when I asked of your negotiations."

Because there were none. But his admission confirms my guess.

"Lord Bailor does not speak for Murwood. Gaining his support will not ensure you get help from any of the others."

How much does Stokerton know of the people here?

How much do you know? According to Aedre, not very much at all.

"They say you've spoken to the mercenary?"

I can feel Thomas tense against me.

"Aye, he's one of many men we've spoken to here," Thomas says.

McGreghere watches me closely.

Stokerton says nothing for a time. But he's the one who breaks the silent stand-off, by saying, "I've neglected to offer our sympathy on the passing of Prince Matteo."

Again, I detect no hint of malice. He seems to mean what he says.

"I would not have expected your sympathy"—given that the ship was headed to Edingham's shores—"but thank you for it."

"An unfortunate turn of events, having Lord Hinton as successor."

I watch for any indication he knows of Aldwine or connects our presence to him, but I see none.

"It is not an ideal situation," I admit. "Much like having Lord Whitley at the queen's heels, I would imagine."

Stokerton's face darkens at the mention of the queen's brother-in-law.

"Just so," he says, drinking.

His companion gives nothing away, nor can I ascertain from the commander how much truth there is to the rumors about the queen's troubles.

"'Tis a shame we are on the brink of war," I offer. And although I am not authorized to do so, I take the opportunity given, especially since Aldwine will not be returning south with me. "Perhaps rather than playing tug-o-war with the Voyagers, we could discuss terms for a truce?"

Thomas nearly spits out his ale. I will have to speak to the man about improving his ability to hide his surprise.

Stokerton puts down his mug and looks me in the eye.

"You've not been given leave to offer such a thing," he states correctly.

"Nay," I admit. "I have not."

He and McGreghere exchange a glance, but it's evident, despite their age difference, Stokerton is the one in charge here.

"Go on then."

I've thought about this quite a bit since learning Stokerton was here in Murwood. My next words carry great risk, but the potential reward makes it worthwhile. Besides, he will learn soon enough of Galfrid's reluctance to name Hinton his successor.

"It is true the king sent nearly two hundred men to your shores. If we'd intended a coup against your queen, I'd have been among them. The intent was a show of force at the border, nothing more."

Can he sense the truth of my words?

"Galfrid recognizes Edingham, as his father did before him."

The rulers of Edingham have always suspected us of secretly wishing to overthrow their "rogue" kingdom. And that may have been true at one time. But now we simply want our people to live in peace.

Unfortunately, Queen Cettina's father did not believe it. As for his daughter, the queen has not been in power for long enough, less than a year, in fact, for her motives to be clear.

"Tsk. Two hundred men to squash a border squabble?"

"It was no squabble, but a brutal slaughter."

McGreghere cuts in. "And now that Meria is weakened because of your tragedy, you wish to make peace?"

"Recall that we are here for the same reason," Thomas says. A reason that has naught to do with peace.

Both men grow silent, thinking, considering.

"Galfrid is reluctant to name Hinton as heir," I admit, "but the man is gathering support from the church. The same church that crosses the border."

Neither kingdom is immune to the meddling of the Prima, his Eldermen, and most importantly, his Shadow Warriors.

"Hinton will be no friend to the queen."

I can tell Stokerton is surprised I've offered so much, but surely he knows the king's nephew well enough to realize I speak the truth.

"Who will Galfrid name instead?"

"I do not know."

Realizing I've lost him, I rush to add, "Truly, I do not know. I left for d'Almerita the day after the sinking."

"To gain the Voyagers' support against us, or against Lord Hinton?"

Neither, but I do not wish to lie to him.

"To know where those in Murwood End stand before we move forward."

A partial truth.

"And you?"

His chin rises defiantly. "The same."

Neither of us will reveal any more. Will it be enough to avoid an all-out war with our neighbors to the east?

"Think on it. We'd planned to leave this very day but can delay until tomorrow."

Which will give me time to talk to Aedre as well.

"What say you?"

Again, he smiles as if he hasn't a care in the world. Since

we last met, the queen's commander has grown bolder, but he's certainly not lost his sense of humor.

"I say we drink and meet again tomorrow, midday."

McGreghere pounds his mug on the table then, a sign of good faith.

I was in the capital of Edingham the first time I saw a Highlander do that. And while some of my companions stared in horror at the men who slammed their mugs down in unison, I admired the gesture. Stokerton joins him, and I smile at the public show of unity. If it is meant to be a warning, as some in Meria suggest, then I am so warned.

But if I'm to drink with my enemy, I might as well get some measure of enjoyment out of it. Since there really is nothing else at the moment to bring me any pleasure.

I failed to convince Aldwine.

And the disastrous way Aedre and I parted . . . I still know not what I will say to her. She seemed quite adamant about not returning to the capital with us. Or marrying me.

My only consolation is the possibility that she will change her mind. Although I hadn't thought to take a wife, I've become more accustomed to the idea of Aedre at court with me.

At home with me.

In my bed, night after night.

And so, I drink.

CHAPTER THIRTY-THREE
VANNI

"My lord, there is someone here to see you."

I ignore the squire, hitting the quintain again and again and again.

I should have gone to the forge earlier, before the tide rose again, but Thomas and I didn't part ways with Stokerton and McGreghere for some time. And how was I to know she would hide from me for a second full day? When her father told me she was still at Nord Manor, I was of half a mind to tell him everything. Demand he send for her. Would he not agree we should marry if he knew the truth?

Restless in my need to strike something, I was almost jealous of the hammer he swung upon his anvil . . . so I decided to come back to the inn to await the opportunity to go to her at Nord Manor.

"My lord?"

I spin toward Christopher, prepared to share my displeasure at being interrupted, when I see the man standing behind him.

"Aldwine."

I drop my sword.

"Why did you not tell me he was here?"

Christopher makes a strangled sound and marches off. I can hear the calls of men coming into port, indicating the end of the day for the fishermen of Murwood End. The end of another day without any communication with Aedre.

"Is she with you?"

Aldwine shakes his head. "Nay."

Which means she is stranded at Nord. Did he take a boat?

"I need to speak to her," I say, without preamble. "Take me back with you."

Aldwine's face is hard. "She does not wish to see you. So, no."

I am liking Galfrid's son less and less.

"I will not leave Murwood End without speaking to her."

He approaches cautiously. "Does your king not anxiously await your return?"

"It matters not to you, as you've made clear." I am angry enough to lash out at the very man I came here to woo.

He shrugs. "You're right. It does not."

My jaw aches from grinding my teeth together so forcefully.

Aldwine leans against the wall of the inn, crossing his arms. "If she were here, what would you say to her?"

I refuse to answer.

"I know about your tryst, d'Abella. And would challenge you because of it if Aedre had not convinced me 'twas her idea."

She told him.

"What did she say to you?"

Before the words are even out of my mouth, I know he will not tell me. The man would no sooner betray Aedre's confidence than he would return with me to claim the throne.

I grit my teeth even harder, biting out, "I would tell her to marry me, that I refuse to leave Murwood End without her."

That Aldwine chuckles infuriates me even further.

"She's right. You do not understand her at all. And that is why she will not see you. Go home. Go back to the king."

The man is actually serious. "Why are you here? Did she send you here to talk to me?"

Again, silence.

"If I do not know her, it's because she will not let me attempt to."

Aldwine shakes his head. "That's where you're wrong, Southerner. Aedre let you in where she denied all others."

I ignore the pain caused by his words.

"I will not leave without at least speaking to her."

Aldwine is quiet for a moment, and then, unexpectedly, he pulls out his sword.

"She says you are a man of honor."

I hold my stance, prepared to fight but not really willing to do so. Not with him.

"I am."

It is the truest statement I've made all day, and nothing I've said today was a lie, even to Stokerton.

"Then give me your word. If I defeat you, you'll respect Aedre's wishes and leave Murwood End without causing her further pain. If you win, I will take you to her straightaway."

There is no decision to make. I will not lose.

"Done."

He puts his sword up. And for a wretched moment, I remember who trained him.

I hear my own mentor's voice in my mind: *A man assured of victory means as little as a man who wishes never to die.*

Albertus would chide me for accepting a challenge with a potential outcome I find unacceptable. But he did not account for the purpose of the challenge being a woman. And for Aedre, I'll not lose.

Aldwine is deft in his initial attack, his training serving him well, and in no time at all, the small courtyard begins to fill with observers. I can sense the presence of my men, likely curious as to the nature of this challenge.

I sidestep his strike, surprised at his skill. Though I anticipated he would disengage, his quick lunge puts me on the defensive.

With blow after blow, the clang of our swords ring out. Without shields, it is a very different fight, blocking impossible. Instead, I catch his strikes by deflecting them. Aldwine does the same. Although I hate myself for it, part of me does hold back. Our swords are not blunted, and it wouldn't bode well to injure Galfrid's son. Nor would Aedre thank me for hurting her friend.

The thought of Aedre finding out I injured Kipp stays with me. It's hard to banish, and so I try to put a quick end to our challenge. It's my downfall. Aldwine takes advantage of a slight slip on my part, and the tip of his sword is pointed directly at my nose before I can fully bring my own down to parry it.

I raise both hands, indicating that I yield.

It is my first loss since my trainer died. Even sickened, the man could anticipate my every move, and only once, in all the years that we trained together, did I ever gain the upper hand.

From my observations, Kipp Aldwine is all his father says of him, and more. A highly skilled swordsman, a man determined to protect those he loves. One who others clearly look up to and support, even if he is a reluctant leader.

On the battlefield, a loss meant death. Here, in this small makeshift training yard, it means something nearly impossible to consider.

"Leave Murwood End, if you are truly a man of your word."

Aldwine puts down his weapon to cheers from his people. I know my own men are behind me, but I do not turn to look at them. Instead, I stare into the eyes of a man destined to be king. How can he not recognize the royal blood that courses through his veins?

"I am, and I will. But I tell you this, Master Aldwine. You were born for the role." I lower my voice. "And I would gladly serve you."

He is unmoved by my declaration.

"If Aedre truly does not wish to see me, tomorrow after my meeting with the queen's commander"—I can hardly believe these words are coming from me—"my men and I will depart for d'Almerita."

Ignoring all around us, I wait for his response.

Aldwine does not hesitate.

"Then I bid you a good day, my lord."

With a quick nod of the head, Aldwine sheathes his sword and turns to leave.

The men surround me, all speaking at once. Incredulous that I lost, effusively praising Aldwine's swordsmanship. My arm burns with the effort of our engagement. I slip my sword back into its sheath.

Salvi repeats the question he and the others continue to ask.

"Why did you fight Aldwine?"

The question finally penetrates, but I can't bring myself to answer it. I am numb with the thought of leaving without seeing her again.

"Vanni?"

All three of my men surround me, and so I give them as much as I'm able.

"He defends Aedre. We leave tomorrow."

Walking away, knowing my answer is insufficient but unable to care, I leave the inn. I walk past the docks and head toward the one place I've found a measure of solace in Murwood End.

CHAPTER THIRTY-FOUR
AEDRE

"*A*edre, you have a visitor."

My heart leaps until I see Kipp in the doorframe.

"You terrified me. For a moment, I thought . . ."

He sits down on the edge of my bed.

"You thought I was d'Abella?"

Sitting up, I shove the doll underneath my pillow. But not quickly enough.

"I see her under there."

Only Kipp could force a smile from me right now.

"Whatever do you mean?"

He's much too quick. Before I can shove him away, Kipp reaches over and snatches the yarn doll out from under the pillow.

"Ah, let me see if I can remember."

He points to her one red arm. "A reminder of the woman's flow and the strength she possesses."

Kipp turns the doll Amma gave me upside down by its foot, its orange leg on display.

"The Garra scorn the church's belief that women are polluted by their desire for sex and are drawn to men as a result of this pollution. Instead, they revel in the belief that we are sexual beings by design, certainly nothing to be ashamed of. And this pink arm is for pleasure, derived from your own hand or another."

I groan and beg him to stop, which only seems to encourage him.

"The yellow leg, a reminder the woman is not an evil temptress or a virginal goddess but can be everything in between, if she so chooses."

He pokes the middle of my yarn Kona directly in the center of the depiction of a dove. "And this, the most important symbol of all. Defiance of the belief that a man and woman cannot find romantic love in marriage."

"Imagine," I scoff, unable to resist, "convening a court to determine such a thing."

Though this "court" ruled in the favor of marital love nearly one hundred years earlier, the vestiges of such a belief are obviously alive and well outside Murwood End.

"You forget in many parts of Meria nobles attempt to retain, or grow, their lands and influence through marriage. Marriage for love is simply not possible for them. And so they rail against the idea of it in every way possible."

"You tell me what I know already, Kipp." I snatch the doll from him, swatting him on the shoulder with my other hand. "Cease your laughing. The Kona is sacred, as well you know."

"And you need no reminders of her lessons. So why does she hide under your pillow?"

I put her back there knowing she's not completely out of his reach.

"She reminds me of Amma."

Kipp sobers immediately. But before he can apologize, I confess, "And I needed a distraction. So I cleaned out the house today and found her among my belongings."

"So?" I ask, unable to wait any longer, the stricken look on his face making me want to change topics. I did not intend to make him feel poorly.

"He believes you are still at Nord. And will not be coming to find you."

Though it is precisely what I asked of him, I feel a pang of disappointment in my chest.

"'Twould be much too painful, speaking to him. Nor do I trust myself when I am around him."

I know it is myself, and not Kipp, I attempt to convince. When I learned Vanni was still in Murwood, so much of me wanted to run to the inn. To find him, hold him. Tell him that I love him and maybe even say the words that would bind us together for life.

I will marry you.

Since yesterday, I've envisioned myself saying that very phrase so many times. Riding from Murwood End with him atop Dex. Sleeping in the same bed and waking up to his face each morn. But I have also imagined the pain I will feel saying goodbye to Father and Kipp and everyone else from home. Spending long days at court with strangers, with Vanni nowhere to be found.

Living with a husband who offered marriage simply out of duty. Who deceived me, even as I know in my heart his interest in me was not solely to get close to Kipp.

Nay, that is not the husband I would have. But still, I cannot keep my mind from wandering. Maybe it will be easier once he leaves?

"What did he say?" I press.

Kipp shrugs. "That he would not leave without speaking to you. And so I challenged him."

I must not have heard him correctly.

"Pardon?"

"Men like him . . . he would not let it go. So I challenged him. He accepted, and lost. So he is leaving, as we agreed."

Only Kipp.

"They say he is an excellent swordsman."

Thank heavens I did not know of this fight when it was happening. I shudder to think of Kipp and Vanni swinging unblunted swords at each other.

"He is."

"And yet you beat him?"

Kipp smiles. "Aye."

"Easily?"

"Nay."

"He leaves now?" I ask, my voice shriller than I would like. I should be relieved. If Vanni set terms with Kipp, he will honor them. And yet . . .

Kipp shifts on the edge of the bed, to sit more comfortably, I presume.

"Tomorrow. Apparently he is to meet with Lord Stokerton again. I've heard they met once already."

"Do you know what they spoke of?"

"Nay."

"Or why they meet again?"

"Nay."

"Ugh."

Kipp chuckles. "Perhaps you should speak to the man yourself. You've enough questions to keep him here until the morrow."

I toss my pillow at him, but Kipp is too quick for me and catches it.

Tomorrow. If I want to see him, there is still time . . .

"How were you able to bring a smile to her face?" my father asks at the door.

Kipp stands, patting the spot from which he'd risen.

"Come and see for yourself. 'Tis not hard. Just ask what she keeps under her remaining pillow."

I make a strangled sound. Kipp knows that while my

father may have built a healing room for me, he does not care for reminders of my training.

Kipp leaves, and my father settles in the spot he vacated.

Knowing he will ask, I pull out the Kona again and show it to him. When he leans toward me, I think he means to take it, but instead, he closes my fingers around the doll, turning my hand into a fist.

"Treasure it, and the memory of Edrys."

I would not have been more surprised had my Amma come back to life and walked into the chamber.

"Father?"

He doesn't move his hand.

"I've failed you, Aedre."

I put my other hand over his, shaking my head.

"Nay, never . . ."

"You are so very much like your mother. And 'tis not a surprise, given your Amma's influence. She would be so proud of you."

All will be well.

"But you still dislike this part of me?"

My father has never looked so . . . vulnerable before.

"I worry for you, maybe overly much, but there is no part of you I dislike. How could there be? Look at the woman you've become."

I feel awful about keeping a secret from him. Perhaps I'll tell him one day, long after Vanni has left. "I've made mistakes," I confess. "I miss Amma so much."

"As do I. But she is still here." He points to my heart.

"Father, do you wish you'd married again? Are you not lonely for companionship?"

He thinks on that and then answers.

"Nay, I am not lonely. I have you and the forge. 'Tis all I need."

It is as I thought. I could never leave Murwood End.

Father needs me, and he would never leave the forge behind. Not that it mattered—I was not going anywhere.

By tomorrow eve, Vanni will be nothing more than a part of my past. A man who swept into Murwood End, captured my heart, and then left me behind to mend it back together.

CHAPTER THIRTY-FIVE
VANNI

"Goddammit man, I don't need your help."

I try again to shove Thomas's hand away, only to stumble up the top stair, cursing.

"Nay? You are sure?"

I remember locking my room, but he opens the door as if by magic.

"How did you do that?"

Thomas lifts up my key.

"Where did you get it?"

He shoves me inside, none too gently. "You gave it to me."

I take off my belt and lay it, and the sword, on a chair next to my bed.

"I hardly think you'll need it this eve," he scoffs. "God help you if you do."

Kicking off my boots, I sit on the bed. Thomas moves his lantern from one hand to the other, the light flashing strangely as if we're out to sea and a thick fog has rolled in.

"I think I'll rest."

Thomas laughs. "Aye, you rest. I'll be up to wake you in the morn."

I focus on my friend rather than the light. "Wake me? I'm no child."

Another chuckle.

Thomas thinks I'm drunk, and maybe I have had too much ale, but I'd still be able to defend us both if called to do so.

"She won't see me."

I haven't said a word of Aedre all eve. As the men ate and drank with those they've come to know in our time here, I skipped the former and concentrated on the latter.

"Aedre?"

"Aye."

"Why won't she see you?"

Maybe I am a bit whittled. I hadn't meant to speak of any of this, but it feels good to unburden myself.

"I brought her back here, just to hold her. Comfort her. Couldn't do it when we sent her Amma out to sea. I didn't mean for it . . . she asked me to . . ."

Thomas shifts the lantern again. It's making me dizzy.

"She was a virgin. But she asked, and I was too weak to say no. And then she ran out. Fled to Nord. To *him*."

Thomas comes closer. Then he's suddenly at eye level.

"Was she the reason you fought Aldwine?"

He's squatting in front of me.

"He said she didn't want to talk to me. I accepted his challenge and lost, and now I'm honor bound to leave without her."

"She clearly cares for you," he says, perplexed. "Why wouldn't she want to see you after she gave herself to you?"

Did she give herself to me? No. Not completely.

"I don't know," I admit. "I told her we would marry."

Thomas coughs. So loudly, I think there might be something wrong with him.

"Are you well?"

"You asked Aedre to marry you?"

"Aye."

And then I think back, as best as I'm able.

"Mayhap I didn't ask. I assumed 'twas already decided."

He makes a sound, stands up, and then pushes me back onto the bed. I let him, only because I am really, really tired.

"You've strange notions of love, Vanni. You do not demand marriage from a woman like Aedre. Though I know her only from afar, 'tis enough to know you are a fool."

Strange notions of love? I have *no* notions of love. My parents died. The king and queen do not love one another. Few at court marry for love.

I know how to wield a sword. How to lead an army of men. How to inspire loyalty in those who follow me. How to be a good subject to the king.

I know many things. But love? The thought is laughable.

I reach out, grab the hilt of my sword to ensure myself it's there.

And then I let the dreamworld take me.

~

"A BARGAIN IS STRUCK, THEN."

Stokerton stands.

We met alone this time. And a good thing, as I'm sick to death of Thomas's snickering. All morn he has kept giving me glances that indicate he knows something I do not. But whenever I've asked him about it, the bastard just laughs.

"You understand I will pursue my purpose here?" Stokerton says, reaching out a hand. "Until we reach an official agreement, we are, in effect, at war."

"If you can convince the Voyagers to fight for the queen, so be it."

For now, an agreement that we will speak to our respective rulers, proposing peace, will have to be enough.

Unlike those we serve, neither Stokerton nor I need to consider the will of noblemen whose power and influence can turn support toward or against us. We've nothing to lose and are therefore in a position to act as righteously as we want. To hope for peace this land has never seen. At least, not since the kingdoms split.

"You will send word?" I ask.

"Aye."

When he smiles, I remind myself this is my enemy. One who's in love with Queen Cettina. He speaks of her as I might . . .

As I might of Aedre.

With adoration.

With reverence.

With love.

As we part, I allow myself to think of Aedre, something I refused to do after Aldwine snatched away my right to see her one last time.

You do not demand marriage from a woman like Aedre.

The last time I drank enough ale to fill the Bay of Sindridge was after Albertus died. Even then, I didn't wake with a sword clutched to my chest the next morn. Still, I can remember pieces of my discussion with Thomas.

"Well?" As if I conjured him, Thomas appears behind me.

"'Tis done." There are too many witnesses around for us to discuss the meeting.

"The innkeeper has offered to serve us a meal as the horses are prepared."

"Go," I tell him. "Take as many provisions as you're able. I will be back by the sixth hour."

Thomas looks at our shadows cast by the sun. "We will be ready."

He looks as if he wishes to say something else, but he simply clasps my shoulder, nods, and turns back to the entrance of the inn.

I'd not planned to leave the inn before our departure. The need for some space, some quiet, some reflection steals over me. My feet move before I can consider where they take me. Away from the village, certainly. Though I know she is still at Nord Manor, I squint at the buildings as I pass them, looking for her.

You do not demand marriage from a woman like Aedre.

And how does Thomas know anything about women like Aedre? There are none like her in Meria. Mayhap none like her here in Murwood End. Climbing these rocks for the last time, I sit on the one we shared, watching as boats come and go. Watching the waves, so predictable yet unpredictable.

For the first time, instead of pushing away thoughts of Matteo and the others clinging to pieces of wood, I let them come. They must have been terrified in those final moments. Although they'd sailed into battle, the warriors among them prepared for what that might mean, falling in battle is a different matter from drowning. They had no chance. No ability to fight for themselves.

Death never used to scare me before. I'd seen from my parents how quickly life could be taken away—and accepted I'd probably lose mine in service to the king. Nay, death never used to scare me, but life . . . that is a different matter entirely.

I do not like you.

Indeed, she did not. With good reason, given her lineage. I wish the Meria her grandmother told her of no longer existed. Many would welcome her, and those who did not . . . could they not learn, as I have?

If a nobleman—a king's man, as she so often said with accusation—could fall in love with a woman who rejects the very king he would give his life to serve, could not others do the same?

Aye, they could—easily—but they will never get the chance.

Just as I will never get the chance to feel her pressed against me again. To touch her, to love her . . . to tell her I am sorry.

Looking up at the sun, I know it is time to leave. Scrambling down from the rocks, I glance one last time at the Cliffs of Murh, trying not to remember the cave Aedre brought me to . . . all while knowing I will never forget. Aedre will never forgive me. But just in case I'm wrong, there's just one more place I need to go before leaving Murwood End for good.

CHAPTER THIRTY-SIX
VANNI

astle d'Almerita, Kingdom of Meria

"Goddammit, Thomas. We leave for Highburn in the morn."

Thomas winks at the woman on his arm, who giggles.

"Look around, my lord. The evening is young. Tomorrow is a wicked master, but it can easily be kept at bay for now."

I do look, the hall as glittering as ever, revelers abounding, despite the ominous promise of tomorrow. Lord Hinton's support has only increased since we've returned, which makes this meeting with him necessary, however it rankles Galfrid. If the next day is a wicked master, it bows to the sun, which will usher it in sooner than Thomas thinks.

"Pay him no mind," he tells the woman, whom I don't recognize. "Lord d'Abella has forgotten how to enjoy himself."

I cannot wholly disagree.

"I will enjoy myself once the matter of King Galfrid's heir has been settled."

By now all at court know the king's nephew is in open rebellion, demanding to be named Galfrid's heir. In response, the king has finally announced his intention to name Lord Calderone as his successor. A distant relative, he is a powerful border lord, though he very rarely attends court. The man is also reluctant to accept, which makes him less than ideal, especially since many blame his inaction as a reason for such violence in the Eastern Marches.

Imperfect, aye.

But a better man than Hinton by far. Unfortunately, too many side with the king's nephew even as they agree he is dangerous. The Prima has put the full weight of the church behind him, and that still means something.

Nor could I have predicted how difficult it would be to return to a life I thought I loved.

"Will you enjoy yourself even then?" Thomas says in parting, a flippant question with a serious edge. Only he knows the full extent of what happened weeks ago with Aedre. And only then because my judgment fled when I drank more than I should have that eve.

Conversation flows around me. I watch the king and his wife, their conversation stilted. Theirs was an arranged marriage, and even after all these years, it shows. With Prince Matteo dead, there is even less binding them.

It stung to inform the king of our failure, but Galfrid admitted he'd expected no different outcome. His words relieved some of my disappointment in myself. But only some. I will never stop blaming myself for my failure with Aedre.

Since returning, I've kept occupied preparing for negotiations with Lord Hinton, attempting to convince Galfrid to treat with Queen Cettina, and training the men for a battle that looks increasingly inevitable.

When my companions attempt to lure me into conversation, I politely turn the conversation back to them. Until one of them, a landed knight with no title whose name escapes me, points toward the entrance of the hall.

I see it at the same time he does, a flash of bright royal blue, as vibrant as the tapestries hanging from every corner of the hall. A latecomer. Indeed, the meal has nearly ended, King Galfrid having just given permission for those present to leave even as he and his queen enjoy the sweetmeats that are, as the king puts it, "his ever-endearing pleasure."

"Who is she?"

From my vantage point, I see nothing but the hem of a blue gown. But whoever has entered the hall must be a stranger to court. Whispers grow louder and then . . .

Nay. It could not be possible.

A rush of excitement, and heat, courses through me as Aedre scans the hall. When I notice Thomas is no longer with his widow but standing by Aedre's side, I realize he must have intercepted her on his way out.

Aedre. Here at court.

Is it possible?

Aye, very possible, given the evidence is there before me. I stand, my legs weak.

She sees me, her eyes locking on mine.

I stride through the hall, reaching her quickly—needing to reassure myself it is indeed her.

"Good evening, Lord d'Abella."

How can she speak so calmly when I cannot even find my voice?

"You are surprised to see me here."

Surprised? The word hardly does justice to what I'm feeling. I look at Thomas.

"I noticed her being escorted to the hall," he says, his companion still nowhere to be found.

My mind works quickly. "Your father told you?"

She nods. "Is there a place where we may speak privately?"

Though she looks beautiful in a gown fit for court, her hair neatly plaited, as is the current style, to me she was just as beautiful when covered in ash from the forge. Or, better yet, nude and lying beneath me.

Even still, it is a surprise to see her like this. And I'm not the only one to notice. We are the center of attention. Even . .
.

I look to the dais and, as expected, Galfrid watches us.

He knows a little about Aedre, those facts which were important for me to relay in terms of Aldwine. He does not know I left my heart behind with her in Murwood.

"By coming here, into the hall, you've made it necessary for me to introduce you," I whisper, knowing of her distaste for the king. "How did you get here? When did you arrive? And this gown . . ."

I guide her to the side of the hall, wishing we were alone.

"Father and I came by ship. We arrived this morn. The gown was a gift from Lady Bailor. She's not visited court in years and warned me it would not be fashionable any longer. But it suits my purposes."

Both king and queen watch us, so I begin to guide her toward them.

"What are those purposes, Aedre?" Her presence here answers my question. But I ask her anyway because I can hardly believe this is happening. "I thought I might never see you again."

I tuck her arm in mine, every step toward Galfrid lighter and more joyous than the one before it.

"Father did not give me the message straightaway. But he did ask many questions. Some easier to answer than others."

"He is here?"

She nods. "Marveling over the chamber he was given. He's vowed never to leave it."

And he never would. If I'm interpreting her presence correctly, this is her home now. Our home.

I'd dwelled on the passage of time over and over and over again. Each day that passed, I became more convinced she would not come.

It was a lot to ask of her.

Forgiveness.

Trust.

Uprooting the only lives they'd known to come to a place that no doubt makes them both uneasy, despite my assurances of their safety.

"And when he gave it?"

"Lord d'Abella," Galfrid booms as we stand before him. "Who is the lovely woman by your side?"

I hesitate, looking at Aedre instead of my liege. By now the hall has quieted. Everyone will be speaking of this for some time.

Aedre looks at me and nods, smiling. Answering my question.

The words I said to her father run through my mind, as they've done so often since I left.

Your daughter asked me to leave Murwood End without seeing her. So I would ask that you deliver her a message. I love her and would marry her. Tell her I am sorry for not sharing my suspicions of her relationship with Kipp sooner. I leave my heart behind, though I do not wish to do so, because it is Aedre's choice to love me back or nay.

He pressed me, of course, for details that were not mine to share.

I refused to say anything more, but I gave him the pin Galfrid had given me in recognition of my post. And I vowed that if he should ever find himself in d'Almerita, there would be a place for him as a castle smith. He could spend his days forging shields and swords instead of nails and hinges.

I ended by telling him, "You will be welcomed into court, where I will gladly be honored to make Aedre my wife."

Assured by her nod, I turn back to the king as Aedre offers a deep curtsy.

"I would introduce you . . ." I remember how she introduced herself to me. Not ashamed of her ancestors but proud. Meria *will* accept her. I will see to it. "I would introduce you to Lady Aedre, daughter of Dal Lorenson, descendant of Athea."

Galfrid does not flinch, but that last bit certainly did not go unnoticed by the crowd at my back. None speak of Athea here, blaming her for having broken the kingdom into two. But that was many, many years ago. And if she broke it, then Meria was fragile indeed.

"And," I add, "my future wife."

I've managed to surprise him.

And Galfrid doesn't like surprises.

CHAPTER THIRTY-SEVEN
AEDRE

"Will that be all, my lady?"

"Aye, thank you."

Though Vanni's bedchamber is dark, the maid has set out enough candles to cast a soft glow. Assuring me of her discretion, Vanni left us, promising to return soon.

This particular wing of the castle is meant for the Curia alone. My father's chamber is so far away, I fear I might never find it again.

I will have to, of course. It would not do well to stay the night here. But I will admit, as I wait for him to return, the excitement of being with him again has helped to push aside any trepidation.

Where is he?

I move to the open shutters, marveling at how much warmer it is here than back home. Or what was my home.

The Kingdom of Meria.

I'd always thought of it as some distant place on the other side of the mountains. And now, Father and I will *live* here.

Father didn't tell me about Vanni's offer at first. Not until I admitted I did indeed love him.

I was miserable after he left. Father and Kipp had to coax me to dress, to eat. I chastised myself for sending him away. For refusing to at least speak with him before he left. My mind was so fixed on him, on our time together, that I could feel him, at times, in the bed beside me.

My misery was such that Kipp finally told my father what he knew about my involvement with Vanni . . . which was when it became clear to Father that my heart was indeed broken, not just from Amma's death, but from losing Vanni. He told me of Vanni's message, of the token he had given him, and tears flowed down my cheeks for a different reason: I knew we would be separated from Kipp. He promised to find a way to see us, however, and Father said we would return to Murwood on occasion too.

We left three days later after a tearful parting with friends, acquaintances, and Agnar, who I will miss dearly. And, of course, Kipp. The journey was an interesting one. I saw things I'd never dreamed of, such as the middle of the ocean with no land in sight, a very different sight than seeing those same waves from the safety of the shore. And through it all, I felt a strong sense of anticipation. Of being with Vanni again. Of kissing him again. Of doing more.

Walking into that hall, I was more nervous than I'd ever been in all my life. Until I saw him.

Then I knew right away I'd made the right decision.

As Amma had said, all would be well.

In d'Almerita.

The door opens. No fur-covered blankets adorn the massive bed inside. Instead, airy curtains give the chamber a very otherworldly feel.

Vanni closes it, turning the key with a click, which announces his intentions clearly. I've thought about this moment so many times that when he reaches me, his hand sliding behind my head, I wonder if this is actually happening.

Without a word, he closes his eyes and kisses me. Tenderly, with a longing and need that I completely understand. The kiss is tentative at first, but it quickly grows deeper. I pour all of my frustration and sadness, my hope and love into him.

When he pulls away, I'm left utterly breathless.

"What took so long?"

"Mmmm," he responds, kissing behind my ear. "I had to make arrangements."

His lips move down my neck, trailing a path of fire in their wake.

"What type of arrangements?"

He stops his ministrations to pull away and look at me.

"We were to leave tomorrow for Highburn Castle, to meet with Lord Hinton."

"Were?"

"Aye. The journey has been delayed for a day." He pauses, looking into my eyes. "For our wedding."

I open my mouth, but before words can come out, he adds, "I've learned my lesson, Aedre. If you would prefer to wait, we'll wait. But I didn't wish to be parted from you for any reason, and things are different here than in Murwood End. I'd not have you travel with me amid whispers of impropriety. Unless you wish it, then whispers be damned. 'Tis your choice, but I would very much like to make you my wife on the morrow. If you'll have me."

I rest my hand on his cheek.

"'Tis what I came here to do. But is it safe, to go to Highburn Castle with you?"

His hand covers mine.

"Aye. I would never put you in danger."

Vanni doesn't wait for my answer. Instead, he spins me

around to face away from him, the move so perfectly executed it's as if he's planned that all eve. I can feel the dress loosening with each tug.

"How did you know it was tied back there?"

His laugh has a dangerous edge. He finishes loosening the ties, slipping my sleeves down ever so slowly. If I thought the anticipation of seeing him again could not be outdone, I was sorely mistaken.

I step out of the dress and reach down to slip off my shoes. When I stand back up, he's behind me again, and I can feel every inch of him.

"How could you have undressed so quickly?"

I try to turn around, but he won't let me. Instead, Vanni presses against me. One hand wraps around to my breast as the other slides up my thigh.

"I've skills you have yet to learn about, Aedre," he whispers in my ear.

And then his hand is there, at the core of me. As is a chair that he apparently moved closer without my noticing.

"I guess you do," I say, referring to his trick with the chair.

"Lift your leg. There."

When I prop one foot on the chair, his fingers enter me fully, his entire length pressing against me from behind.

"Tomorrow we wed," he says, his breath tickles my ear. "But tonight I make you mine, Aedre."

Last time, the pressure built and built until it finally spilled over. This time, maybe because the anticipation has been building for so long, I begin to shudder almost immediately.

When I look down to see his bare arm around me, strong and sure, the tremors intensify. With the same deftness that saw him disrobing so quickly, he lifts my shift over my head, moving us toward the bed.

Once on it, Vanni lies back and pulls me on top of him.

"You are in control as much as I am," he says, reaching up to touch me just about everywhere. I've never felt so . . . worshipped. "In bed and out of it."

I get into a more comfortable position, knowing how this works even though I've not yet experienced it.

I am, after all, a Garra. So, reaching down, I stroke Vanni as if I'd done so many times before. His moans of pleasure encouraging, I guide him toward me. Seeing me struggle, Vanni lends his help, sinking in deeper and deeper.

This time, there is no pain.

Propped up with my hands on his chest, I revel in the feeling of finally being joined with him again. Revel in . . .

"Oh!"

Vanni grabs my hips, pulling down. We move in rhythm, the feeling entirely different than it was the first time. It's just as good, though, maybe even better. When his lips part, his eyes rolling back in pleasure, I feel more powerful than I've ever been.

This is why the Garra have been hunted. Mocked. Ridiculed. Even killed.

Every moan that escapes from Vanni encourages me until our movements verge on frantic. His hips thrust up from the bed as I circle him, so close . . .

"Vanni." My voice is breathless.

"Aye, love. Come for me."

I let go then, screaming both from the incredible release and the gift my soon-to-be husband has given me. I am in charge. His guttural cry follows mine as his fingers dig into the flesh of my hips. I welcome the sensation, collapsing atop him.

Vanni flips me then, though we are still joined. His smile is a teasing one.

"I am an overly sexual creature, and thoughts of you

occupy me too often. Perhaps you can help with that affliction."

"I've heard those words before," I say through laughter. He kisses my neck, then trails kisses down to my breast, taking it into his mouth. Circling and teasing the nipple, I can feel him harden already even though I know such a thing is scarcely possible.

"We just—" My words are cut off by a kiss unlike any we've shared before. Not slow, not careful, but hard and eager. Our tongues tangle as he begins to move. Before long, his full length fills me as we repeat the dance that I've only just learned.

This time is shorter but no less intense as my hands attempt to grasp his wide shoulders. He wraps my legs around him, and we come together as one.

For tonight.

For forever.

EPILOGUE
AEDRE

"**M**y hand is slipping," I call up to him, but Vanni pulls me atop Dex as effortlessly as he did back in Murwood. This time we ride north, to Highburn Castle. To meet with the man who is attempting to take Meria from his uncle.

"I would never drop you," he says, pulling me onto his lap. "Did I not tell you that?"

I settle in front of him, remembering his words clearly.

"Aye, you did, husband."

He leans forward to kiss me just below my ear, something that surprises me given his men are with us, but none of them seem to notice or care.

"Are outward shows of affection not frowned upon here?"

I may never have been to the capital before but am well aware of their customs. There is a strict code of conduct here, and kissing your wife publicly is frowned upon.

"You are a Voyager, are you not?"

"Aye," I agree as we begin to move. "But this is certainly not Murwood End."

Our entire village could likely fit inside the courtyard of Castle d'Almerita.

"A pity. There's much I came to love there, though I can't remember being so enamored with it on my previous visit."

Smiling, I turn to look at him.

"Do you ever wonder if our paths crossed then? When you were there as a child? I often spent time escaping the forge to watch ships come into port."

One of the men calls out to Vanni. He answers and then turns his attention back to me. Of the twenty or so people assembled for the journey, I am the only woman.

"I have thought of that. And also of our first meeting . . . you said you did not like me."

I watch the courtyard, teeming with activity, as we leave and pass through the inner ward.

"I did not like what you represented," I correct him. "Do you really believe I will be welcomed here in Meria?"

Our hastily arranged wedding, with the king in attendance no less, was nonetheless much more opulent than I'd ever expected my wedding to be. Surrounded by glittering gold and warm colors. But Father was there, and Vanni, of course, and that's what mattered.

We ride past the gatehouse now, its walls so thick I cannot imagine them ever being penetrated, and into the open fields. The land is flat here, another thing that will take some getting used to. I was raised with a view of the Northern Loigh Mountains surrounding us, but here, you could see for miles, the city center off to the right but still visible.

We veer in the opposite direction.

"Lady Edrys lived in a different time," he says gently. "There may still be some resistance from the church, but we'll navigate that together."

Which reminds me.

"I never did see Father Beald again after Lord Bailor's. I wonder what happened to him?"

Vanni makes a sound behind me. "Do not wonder about him overly much. The man hardly deserves it."

I wiggle my bottom, attempting to get more comfortable, when Vanni groans.

"Do not do that, wife."

His words are harsh, but his tone is not. And precisely because he told me not to, I do it again. "You mean this?"

Growling, he leans into me and whispers into my ear. "You're unaccustomed to riding, and no doubt your backside will be sore by the time we stop. Keep that up, Aedre, and I cannot guarantee I will take that fact into consideration."

Because I've been bold these last two nights, and he's rewarded me well for it, I lean back and say, "Then 'tis good it will not be my backside you find pleasure in this night."

His arms tense around my waist.

"Aedre," he warns.

"And thankfully there are many ways a man and woman can find pleasure. I believe you are familiar with some of them, but there are others, forbidden by the church, of course, that I would like to explore." I may not have tried them, but I know of them.

His face is suddenly buried in my neck.

"You are a temptress."

I turn toward him, finding his lips easily. As we canter along, Vanni's mouth covers mine. His tongue slashing, tasting. Until the men begin to holler.

Laughing, I straighten myself once again.

"You worried once about having a wife, a distraction," I muse, not wanting to ruin the moment but also curious about Vanni's change in thinking.

"I've solved that problem easily enough. You will come

with me everywhere I go. Though your knife skills might need some honing."

I like that idea.

"Even into battle?"

Though I'd said it in jest, Vanni suddenly becomes quiet. When I spin around in the saddle, he's regarding me with a curious look.

"I fear you've come to the capital at a more eventful time than I'd like. There may be battles ahead, Aedre. And no, you'll not be coming to them. But I vow to you . . ."

He holds his chin high, reminding me of the proud man I first approached on the docks of Murwood End, an outsider who nonetheless stood his ground.

"Whatever happens in the days ahead, I will protect you and your father as fiercely as I will the king. You accused me once of loving him more than anyone, but I give you this truth. *You* taught me to love."

That he mentions Father too . . .

"I love you, Vanni."

"And I love you, Aedre." He kisses me on the nose, and I settle in for a long day's journey.

All will be well, indeed.

Not ready to leave Vanni and Aedre just yet? Download a bonus chapter to stay with them just a bit longer and receive updates on the next book in the series at:

https://pixelfy.me/KingsBonus

ALSO BY CECELIA MECCA

ORDER OF THE BROKEN BLADE

The Blacksmith
The Mercenary
The Scot
The Earl
The Chief

BORDER SERIES

The Ward's Bride: Prequel Novella
The Thief's Countess
The Lord's Captive
The Chief's Maiden
The Scot's Secret
The Earl's Entanglement
The Warrior's Queen
The Protector's Promise

The Rogue's Redemption
The Guardian's Favor
The Knight's Reward
Box Set 1 (Books 1-3)
Box Set 2 (Books 4-6)

TIME TRAVEL & PARANORMAL

Enchanted Falls

Falling for the Knight

Highlanders Through Time

Sexy Scot
Scandalous Scot

ABOUT THE AUTHOR

Cecelia Mecca is the author of medieval romance and sometimes wishes she could be transported back in time to the days of knights and castles. Although the former English teacher's actual home is in Northeast Pennsylvania where she lives with her husband and two children, her online home can be found at CeceliaMecca.com. She would love to hear from you.